Treasure
and
Redemption

Here's what readers are saying about "Of Chains and Slavery."

"Commander Johnson has given us an intriguing and fast-paced adventure page-turner that should be on every high schooler's required reading list; weaving together the warp of pre-revolution history with the woof of classic pirate fiction to fashion a master tapestry describing the complicated and brutal life of this new swashbuckling hero, Joshua Smoot. This novel cries out to become a major motion picture."

Doug Hawley, Owner of "Ye Landmark Collectibles" of Poulsbo, WA

"Master storyteller Roger Johnson takes us on an incredible adventure as we follow Joshua Smoot from his kidnapping from Savannah to his ultimate life as a pirate in search for the legendary Treasure of Dead Man's Chest. *"John Flint's Bastard"* has it all; high adventure, treachery, honor, gasping emotion, white-knuckled drama, all wrapped in a suspenseful story line that will not let you go. Well done, Commander Johnson!"

Robert Ceccarini, NYPD Detective Lieutenant

"An exciting adventure that transports you to another time and place. Well researched and explained. I look forward to reading more by Commander Johnson."

Joe Marek, Merrick's Privateers

"It was a genuine pleasure reading *"John Flint's Bastard."* It is an exciting blend of history and fiction during the end of the Age of Piracy and the beginning of the Age of Liberty. Make room Blackbeard, Billy the Kid, and Captain Hook, because there's a new Swashbuckler named Joshua Smoot riding the high seas."

Wade John Taylor, editor, The Pamphlet

"If you love America, you will love *"John Flint's Bastard, Slavery and Revenge,"* and the third book in this pirate adventure trilogy, *"Treasure and Redemption."* Commander Johnson spins a compelling yarn that takes place just before the American founding, and introduces us to a new swashbuckler named Joshua Smoot. A true page-turner that I could not put down. I look forward to part three."

Corey Millard, avid reader of pirate adventure

"A brilliantly painted canvas of the by-gone Golden Age of Piracy and the introduction of Joshua Smoot! Filled with intrigue, suspense, and both joyful and bitter raw emotion; Commander Johnson weaves a tale of the destiny of souls that will stir the hearts of all that read their way into this epic story! I highly recommend the trilogy!"

Penny Caldwell, author, "The God of the Mountain."

"As a child, I read and re-read Treasure Island and have hungered all these decades to learn the ultimate destination of Long John Silver and the rest of that famous treasure. That hunger has now been satisfied in Commander Johnson's trilogy, *"Of Chains and Slavery."* Written in the classic style of Robert Louis Stevenson, this fast-moving pirate novel follows the complicated life and adventures of John Flint's bastard—Joshua Smoot—from his kidnapping at Savannah, through his years as a slave, and finally to his quest for the Treasure of Dead Man's Chest. A must read for those who share my hunger."

Scott C. Kuesel, Wisconsin Maritime Historical Society

"How important is a man's identity, and what is he willing to sacrifice to keep it? These are the life-changing decisions young Joshua Smoot—the bastard son of the notorious pirate John Flint—must make. Will his odyssey break him or will he find the courage, strength, and faith to survive and conquer the life he's been forced into? The *"Of Chains and Slavery"* trilogy is a wild ride and a must read."

Michael Carver, Historical Interpreter and Reenactor

Treasure and Redemption

Of Chains and Slavery

~

A Trilogy: Part Three

Roger L. Johnson
Commander, USN

SEAWORTHY PUBLICATIONS, INC. • MELBOURNE, FLORIDA

Treasure and Redemption
Of Chains and Slavery, A Trilogy: Part Three
Copyright ©2025 by Roger L. Johnson
Commander, USN
ISBN: 978-1-948494-98-4
Published in the USA by:
Seaworthy Publications, Inc.
6300 N Wickham Rd.
Unit #130-416
Melbourne, FL 32940
Phone 321-389-2506
e-mail orders@seaworthy.com
www.seaworthy.com

Library of Congress Cataloging-in-Publication Data

Names: Johnson, Roger L., Commander, author.
Title: Treasure and redemption / Roger L. Johnson, Commander, USN.
Description: Melbourne, Florida : Seaworthy Publications, Inc., 2024. |
    Series: Of chains and slavery, a trilogy ; part 3 | Summary: "If you are
    like me, you read Robert Luis Stevenson's Treasure Island several times
    as a child, and have wondered what happened to Long John Silver, Benn
    Gunn, and The Treasure of Dead Man's Chest. You now hold in your hands
    the third novel in the Of Chains and Slavery trilogy, which answers
    those nagging questions. True to his nature, Long John Silver was able
    to lead, coerce, and manipulate many of the men who fought the American
    Revolution to unknowingly do his bidding, even General George Washington
    and John Paul Jones-all during a twenty-month period in which the naval
    hero disappeared from history. You will watch Pirate Captain Joshua
    Smoot's life transition as successes and failures twist and reshape him
    into the man that destiny had always intended. You will also discover
    what happened to Long John Silver, what happened to the treasure, and
    what happened to Rebecca Keyes-Joshua's betrothed who was forced to
    banish him into slavery"-- Provided by publisher.
Identifiers: LCCN 2024015570 (print) | LCCN 2024015571 (ebook) | ISBN
    9781948494984 (paperback) | ISBN 9781948494991 (epub)
Subjects: LCGFT: Action and adventure fiction. | Sea fiction. | Novels.
Classification: LCC PS3610.O3753 T74 2024 (print) | LCC PS3610.O3753
    (ebook) | DDC 813/.6--dc23/eng/20240404
LC record available at https://lccn.loc.gov/2024015570
LC ebook record available at https://lccn.loc.gov/2024015571

DEDICATION

I affectionately dedicate this "Of Chains and Slavery" trilogy to my wife and soul mate, Elizabeth, who has patiently endured the many months required to research and record this epic adventure of the Pirate Captain Joshua Smoot.

TABLE OF CONTENTS

PREFACE

On November 14, 1493, Spanish explorer Christopher Columbus stepped ashore onto what he called Santa Crux—Spanish for Holy Cross—and was immediately attacked by the Kalinago tribe—a native clan that inhabited a nearby river valley on the northern coast of the island. This was the first of many battles fought between the invading Spaniards and the indigenous tribes that inhabited the string of Caribbean islands. During the early 16th century, Saint Croix—as it was later named—traded dominion between the English, the French, and the Dutch.

In 1725, Saint Thomas Governor Frederick Moth entered negotiations with France, and on June 15, 1733, France and Denmark signed a treaty with the Dutch West Indies Company to purchase this prominent island. Moth immediately established a port for the exportation of sugar and cotton to Europe and became Saint Croix's first Governor. In 1754, after eleven years of local rule, King Frederick of Denmark took control of Saint Croix. At this time, the white population of the island was approximately four-hundred while the slave population reached nearly eight-thousand. With the ascension of King Christian VI of Denmark to the throne, Moth's port town was named Christiansted.

A short distance to the northeast of Christiansted lies a small island that the pirates called Dead Man's Chest—a piece of inhospitable earth with neither animal life nor a reliable water supply. Fed only by the occasional rains, the vegetation on the twelve-furlong island consisted of Sea Grass, spiny cactus, sparse groves of Acacia, and a half dozen poisonous Manchineel trees whose white sap burned the careless man's skin like lye. The perfect place to hide a treasure.

Joshua Smoot was born to David and Elaine MacBride on January 29, 1748. During that same year, two pirate captains—Andrew Murray sailing the brig *King James*, and John Flint sailing the Brigantine *Walrus*—joined forces to intercept and take captive the Spanish Galleon, *Santissima* Trinidad as it passed through the Windward Passage. The galleon was said to be carrying approximately L1,500,000 in gold, silver, and jewels from Panama to Cadiz, Spain. The attack went as planned, and when the treasure was counted, it came to just over L2,200,000. By agreement with Captain Flint, the treasure was to be split in three equal shares of L700,000. One share to John Flint, one share to Andrew Murray, and the third share to Colonel O'Donnell to support the flagging Jacobite rebellion. Captain Murray—also known as Captain Rip Rap—kept the extra L100,000 aboard the *Royal James*, and took the other two shares to the Dead Man's Chest where his grandnephew, Robert Ormerod, Colonel O'Donnell, and the colonel's daughter, Moira were left for nearly a week to bury the dozens of casks and chests. Some weeks later at Savannah, the colonel was killed by John Flint, leaving Robert and Moira the only two to know where the L1,400,000 was buried. At their marriage some months later in New York City, Moira insisted that Robert covenant to God that he would never reveal the location of the Treasure of Dead Man's Chest.

CHAPTER ONE:

Henry Morgan's Secret

J ust as the rope that seaman Parker tied between the anchor and Joshua's foot was meant to end his life in the depths of Baracoa Bay that day many years before, Governor Wright's refusal to grant him his Letter of Marque had finally scuttled Joshua's prospects of becoming an American Privateer. But now, with Henry Morgan's unexpected arrival at High Tortuga and his announcement that the American's were building two disguised and armed frigates for their quest for the treasure of Dead Man's Chest, everything had changed.

As Joshua filled their two glasses with rum, Sarah Smoot stepped to the study with a tray of tea and sweet cakes. She stopped and made a quick survey of the room. "I heard yelling, and I don't see Governor Wright." She looked at the red-headed youth. "You're Henry Morgan, aren't you?" She gave Joshua a questioning glance and turned back to the young man. "What are you doing here?"

"Aye!" Henry stood, gave a theatrical wave of the bloody towel, followed by a deep bow. "'Tis me—Henry Morgan—forgiven of all my sins and in the flesh!"

"Where is Governor Wright?" She nodded toward the stack of money. "And, whose blood is that?"

"It's mine." Henry held up his hand. "Joshua stabbed me when I tried to take it."

Joshua put the tip of his dirk to the pile of money. "The Governor is gone and everything has changed."

Sarah set down the tray and gave Joshua a scolding mother's look. "You told me that if you ever saw Henry again, you'd shoot him for something that happened in New York." She turned and looked toward the front door. "For starters, shall I assume that Governor Wright refused your bribe?"

"Yes, and…" Joshua looked at Henry and back to her. "A lot has changed."

"You already said that, Joshua." She turned to Henry. "What about you? Can you explain any of this?" When Henry didn't answer, she looked to Joshua. "You never told me what happened in New York—only that you needed to kill Henry."

"Things went bad in New York."

"How bad?"

"I already told you the part about Long John Silver trading maps with me—his to the grave of John Flint and mine to the location of a treasure on Dead Man's Chest."

"Where is Dead Man's Chest."

"It's a small island off the north coast of Saint Croix."

"Okay, get back to New York."

"When we arrived, we docked *Seacrest* and I sent Henry ahead to Robert Omerod's home posing as a messenger boy."

"I delivered a note asking Mister Ormerod if he would meet with John Manley—the name Joshua was using."

"We had our meeting that afternoon, and he suspected that Long John Silver sent me." Joshua gave a grimace. "He chased me off at gun point."

"So, get to the part that made you want to kill Henry."

"I came up with the plan that if we could take is little girl hostage, we could force him to mark and sign John Silver's map to get her back."

"How old is this little girl?"

"She was four."

"What do you mean, was?" Sarah looked at Joshua. "What did you two do to her?"

"We followed her and her nanny to the park, and while Henry created a distraction, I kidnapped her."

"Oh, Lord!"

"Henry was to hold her at a sail shed near *Seacrest* while I went back to get John Silver's map marked and signed."

"Did he?"

"He signed and dated it, but as he was getting ready to make the mark, there was a commotion outside." He looked at Henry. "Henry was standing in the middle of the street with Jane's burned body lying at his feet."

"Burned?" She turned to Henry. "How could that happen while you were watching her?"

"A girl named Daisy came to the shed with a bottle of rum and told me that my friend rented us a room for us." Henry looked at Joshua. "I believed her."

"My God!" She turned to Joshua. "Why would you do such a thing?"

"I didn't do it."

"Then who did?"

"I'm thinking that Robert Ormerod must have had an enemy in New York who was watching what Henry and I did, and took advantage of it by sending that prostitute to distract him."

"Then that explains why you carry that loaded pistol everywhere. You're waiting for the Yorkman's assassin to show up to kill you."

"I was only gone for half a glass, Sarah. When I got back my lamp was turned over and little Jane was dead."

"So, there stands Henry in the middle of the street over the Yorkman's dead little girl." She studied them for a long moment. "Why didn't he shoot you two on the spot?"

"He tried, but I ran one way and Henry ran the other way."

"So, that was the last time you two saw each other until today?"

"I tried to go back to *Seacrest*, but Joshua shot at me."

"So back to my first question. Why are you here, Henry, and why haven't you shot him yet, Joshua?"

Henry looked at Joshua. "Is it safe to tell her?"

"She'll find out whether we tell her or not."

"Okay." Henry turned to her. "After New York, I wondered about for a while living off my pickpocketing. Then I got me a job as a carpenter and painter at the Forrestal Ship Company in Charles Town until Robert Ormerod showed up and I had to run away."

"What was he doing there?"

"That's why I'm here, Miss Sarah. Alex Forrestal is finishing two identical disguised warships and they are both named *Silver Cloud*."

"Why?" She looked to Joshua. "What do two warships in Charles Town have to do with the death of that little girl in New York?"

"I'll tell her." Joshua stroked the scar on his face. "Do you remember when I left in *Seacrest* and returned a month later in *Le Tiburon*?"

"I remember it well, because you were in a rotten mood for about the longest time."

"During that voyage, I took a merchantman captive, and because I had promised him, I took it to Charles Noble at King's Town. After he traded *Le Tiburon* to me for *Seacrest*, one of my men told me that there were a thousand cannons hidden under the ballast stones of that merchantman."

"And then you did something that got your rudder shot off. Tell me about that."

"I found out that Charles' son was sailing to Fredericksburg in a postal packet, so I decided to kidnap him to get my cannons back."

"Kidnapping is becoming a habit with you, isn't it Joshua?"

"Long story short—Henry learned that one of Forrestal's ships is sailing to Kings Town while the other one is sailing to Dead Man's Chest to retrieve a large Spanish treasure."

"Let me guess." Sarah studied the two. "Legend has it that Long John Silver has been waiting for the opportunity to get that treasure for over two decades, and somehow he's involved in every aspect of this."

"That may be, Sarah, but whether he is or not, it doesn't change our plans."

"You and Henry have a plan to get that treasure?"

"We were just about to put one together when you stepped to the door."

"Hmm." Sarah took a seat and turned to Henry. "Tell me what you know."

"Well, the first thing is that Captain Alan Steele is departing from Charles Town in the privateer *Eagle* in a week."

"He's going ahead to Dead Man's Chest?"

"As I understand it, his mission is to make sure there are no enemy ships waiting for the *Silver Cloud*, to protect her while her crew retrieves the treasure, and then to escort her to a rendezvous with the other *Silver Cloud* where they will trade crews and go their separate ways."

"Do you know how many men will be on the *Eagle* and the *Silver Cloud*?"

"Fifty and a hundred." Henry looked to Joshua and back to Sarah. "Why?"

"How many crewmen could you sail with if you departed in the morning, Joshua?"

"Right now, I have about sixty men, give or take a few."

"That would put you at Christiansted before the *Eagle*. What would you do then?"

"Uh…" Joshua looked at Henry and back to Sarah. "Like Henry said, we were about to come up with a plan when you showed up."

"Okay." She fell silent.

After a minute, Joshua touched her arm. "Do you have an idea what we should do?"

"Wait!" She ran a finger in a small circle on the desk for a minute. "I'm thinking." The tree sat silent while she moved her fingers about the desk. Finally, she looked up at Joshua.

"What?"

"If you sailed tomorrow, you would there—to Christiansted—before the *Eagle*."

"Yes?"

"Is there a way you could take her captive?"

"If we could catch her at sea, we might be able to sink her, but those privateers are good fighters. We could be sunk if things go bad."

"No, not a sea battle, Joshua."

"Then what?"

"Think of the advantage it would give you Joshua, if you could kidnap the *Eagle*'s entire crew and replace them with your men."

"Ah-ha!" Joshua looked at Henry. "I told you my sister was a clever one, didn't I?"

"Aye." Henry looked at Sarah. "How many men should we take on *Le Tiburon*?"

"At least a hundred and fifty."

"Then we're going to have to find a hundred more men as quickly as we can."

"I can get the word out fast, Joshua. Tell me what to say and I'll have all the men we'll need lined up at *Le Tiburon* tomorrow morning."

"Wait." Sarah got a tablet and a quill. "How large is this Spanish treasure supposed to be?"

"Captain Van Mourik told me that it's a million and a half."

"So…" Sarah made a quick calculation and looked up. "Woof!"

"What?"

"If you divide one-hundred and fifty into a million and a half, that comes out to ten-thousand per share." She looked at Henry.

Henry gave Joshua a grin. "That would make your share and mine fifty-thousand each."

"Here's what you tell them, Henry. *Le Tiburon* is sailing in a week to dig up a huge treasure, and each man will bring home five-thousand dollars."

Early the next morning, several hundred men gathered at the windmill to vie for a crew position on *Le Tiburon*.

CHAPTER TWO:
The Injured Eagle

With her cleaner lines and earlier departure from Charles Town, the *Eagle* was well ahead of her ward, the *Silver Cloud*. She arrived at Christiansted harbor in the late afternoon and crept amidst the dozens of other vessels that cluttered the harbor. Flying her French flag, the corvette *Le Tiburon*, was well-hid from Captain Alan Steele and his lookouts.

"On deck!" Henry Morgan pointed at the approaching ship. "That's the *Eagle*!" Henry dropped his spyglass into its leather sheath and slid down one of the lines to the deck. "She's here, Cap'n, just like I told you she'd be!"

"Are you certain that's her?"

"Aye, Cap'n." He pointed. "I did some work on her just before I left for Savannah."

"Well, well." Smoot studied the new arrival. "It looks like you might be earning your five shares after all."

While they watched, the *Eagle* luffed her main and jib, and dropped her larboard anchor, putting her approximately three hundred yards seaward of *Le Tiburon*. An hour later, when two-thirds of the crew would normally have gone ashore for liberty, a lone ship's boat with but three men aboard pulled slowly to the dock just aft of the pirate ship.

"Hmm." Joshua handed the spyglass to Henry. "Is that Captain Steele at the tiller?"

Henry gave a nod as he looked through the instrument. "Aye. That's him alright." He gave his captain a squint and an outstretched hand. "We had a bet, remember?"

Smoot gave the lad an angry stare for three seconds and then pulled the agreed prize from his pocket. "Here!"

"It's only fitting, Captain, since you made me pay you the ten quid back in Savannah." Henry's eyes were fixed on the shiny gold coin that promised another night of good grog and female companionship.

"That was a fair bet, Morgan, and you lost." Smoot flipped the coin high into the air toward the mizzenmast, sending Henry in a mad scramble across the deck as the coin rolled toward a waiting scupper. When he returned with his prize, he noticed that Joshua was deep in thought. "Is something wrong?"

"I was just counting on most of the *Eagle*'s crew being ashore tonight in the taverns, that's all."

"It's still early. Maybe Captain Steele wants to find a tavern where it's safe for his men to spend their money."

"No, he's doing what I would do in his place."

"What's that?"

"He was sent here with a single mission—to protect the *Silver Cloud* from pirates. That means he isn't going to take the chance of letting his crew tell anybody in Christiansted about the *Silver Cloud* or the treasure on Dead Man's Chest." Joshua looked to the *Eagle*. "We'll just have to change our plans a little to make up for this."

"Change our plans?" Henry stuck a finger in his ear and gave a twist. "If he isn't gonna let them come ashore, then how are we gonna take the *Eagle* from him?"

"I have an idea."

An hour later, Joshua, Henry, and four of their men found Captain Steel at Hubbard's Dock. "Henry, I want you to stand watch on Captain Steele while our men take his two crewmen captive."

"Where are you going?"

"I have some business to attend to at the Three Bells Tavern. It should only take me half a glass."

"What if Steele comes out while you're gone?"

"Hold him at gunpoint and come get me."

It took Joshua a little longer than he expected, but Steele was still in Hubbard's office when he returned. "Is he still inside?"

"Aye. They're inside that small office at the starboard side of the warehouse. From what I could hear, they're haggling over the high prices of the provisions."

"Okay, listen up." He turned to the four crewmen. "Henry and I will go inside to get Captain Steele. I want you four to stand just outside the door with your pistols drawn."

"Do you want us to shoot them if they run for it?"

"No. I need Captain Steele alive."

"What about the other two?"

"I don't need them, but I do need Steel."

The six walked across the warehouse floor to the office where they heard Captain Steele arguing. Joshua stopped and whispered. "Stand here—two on each side."

"You're charging me double what I paid at Hispaniola for the dried beef." Alan Steele pulled back his money. "I'll not pay eight pounds per barrel."

"But you're forgetting that I have to pay for shipping and storage costs, and the buccaneers of Hispaniola sold it to you right there where they kill the cattle and dry their flesh." His hand moved an inch toward the money. "If you wanted it at the buccaneer's price, you should have bought it there."

"I would have, but I didn't have time—" The door behind Captain Steele pulled open.

"Captain Steele, I presume?" Joshua and Henry stepped into the small office and blocked the door.

"Aye?" Steele turned and looked up at Joshua. "Do I know you?"

"We've never met, but you were told to watch for me."

"Who are you? What do you want?"

"I'm Pirate Captain Joshua Smoot." He offered his hand. "I'm here to take the Treasure of Dead Man's Chest."

"Damn!" Steele jumped to his feet and put his hand on his pistol.

"You are now my prisoner." Joshua turned to Henry. "Take his pistol, escort him to the warehouse, put him in irons with his men, and wait for me."

"Where are you going, Captain? I thought you wanted to question him."

"I'll be there shortly, after I speak with the ladies that are waiting for me at dockside."

"What ladies?"

"You'll see." Joshua turned and strode across the dock to where a large group of gayly-dressed women waited in a long boat. "You there!" He pointed at the woman with the red hair. "You've got my money, but just so I know that you understand what you're supposed to do when you reach the *Eagle*, tell me again."

"This!" She reached into her bodice and pulled out a small, rolled parchment. "We row to the *Eagle* and hand this to whoever is in charge. Then, we go aboard with these six casks of rum, and have a party."

"Alright." Joshua put a foot on the longboat and gave a shove. "Go."

☠ ☠ ☠

The *Eagle*'s watch saw the launch first. "Mister Todd, sir!"

"What is it?"

"We've a boat full of ladies approaching from Hubbard's Dock!"

"Oh?" The first officer closed the logbook and walked quickly toward the rail where the agitated young seaman stood pointing. "They're still so far out." Todd shaded his eyes against the afternoon sun. "What makes you think its ladies?"

"Look how they're pullin' them oars an' meandering about the bay, sir. That's gotta be ladies or children, an' they're much too big fer children!"

Most of the other crewmen were quicker on their feet than the first officer, and were already crowding and shoving for a spot along the rail.

"Back away there!" Todd moved toward the bow and pressed himself between two of his crew. It was just as the watch had reported. A dozen women. "Well, I'll be!"

The liberty-starved sailors barely heard his orders for their hooting and hollering at the approaching women. The shifting breeze brought the full impact of the lady's sweet fragrances across the water, up over the bow and along the ship to the forty-seven waiting noses. The perfumes were mostly cheap, but the sailors were more interested in where the lotions had been applied than with their value. Todd was a man of similar desires but duty to his captain and their mission prevailed.

"You there!" Todd called out in a stern voice while the crew watched the boat circle around to the leeward side of the *Eagle*. "In the boat! Standoff, and state your business!"

The bovine blond stood carefully to her feet and shaded her eyes with a woven cane fan. It wasn't that she was actually better endowed than her companions but rather that she had paid her dressmaker better than the rest. She called back to Todd in a bubbly voice. "Captain Steele sent us!"

There arose a cheer from the crew for their absent captain. When the yelling finally subsided and two sailors had been fished from the warm bay, Todd continued his interrogation of the visitors.

"And what evidence do you offer us, young lady?"

"This, sir!" She reached between her generous breasts and searched for something. "It's a note from Captain Steele." The entire crew sucked in its breath as one man. She extracted the small, rolled parchment tied with a crimson ribbon. The eleven other ladies giggled as the lusty sailors exhaled together and let out a second cheer.

The sailor next to Todd began to climb over the rail.

"Not so fast, MacPherson!" He reached out and caught the eager seaman by the rope that held up his britches.

"By yer leave, sir! I was just goin' fer the note!" There was another round of laughter and catcalls from both vessels.

"Well, go ahead then." While the crew sent up another cheer, Todd released the rope allowing the youth to leap to the bottom rung of the ship's ladder with the agility of a monkey. "But mind you MacPherson, touch nothing but the captain's note!"

Todd knew that if he was not extremely careful, he could lose the entire crew on the spot. MacPherson was back in a moment with the note between his teeth. He held it up to the crew and twirled about with the prize. Todd held out his hand. "MacPherson! May I?"

Todd read it to himself:

Jason:

I have reconsidered the present situation and have decided that the men deserve some female companionship. Since they cannot come ashore, I have decided to send these twelve women to the ship. Please take these ladies aboard for the evening, along with the refreshments they convey. I may be detained ashore with Mister Hubbard longer than usual, but I expect to be back before the ladies are gone. If not, have them escorted back to the dock tomorrow morning at first light.

A. Steele

Captain: Privateer Eagle

Todd studied the signature for a moment. There was something different about it, but his baser nature prevailed. He turned and looked down at the ladies. Any suspicion was forced aside by the temptation awaiting him at the water line.

"Bosun! You may bring the ladies aboard!"

The crew exploded in cheers and praises for their captain and first officer. Within minutes, the ladies were on deck with their six casks of rum, and both quickly disappeared below deck. The first two mugs of rum were brought to Todd and the bosun. The men cast lots, and those who would have to wait on deck for their turns with the women made a sport of outdoing one another in toasting their absent captain and throwing their dirks at the mainmast.

Todd sat on one of the cat's heads with his rum and called aft at his crew. "I'm sure our captain would appreciate your enthusiasm, but the women are to be put ashore before sunrise. And mind you, I'll see to it personally that any man caught fighting will find himself in irons." Nobody heard him.

Within an hour, every sailor had enjoyed their first time with a lady, and there were no fights. As the crew waited for their second encounter, they took to the rum and joined the knife games. Before the sun set, every sailor was fast asleep, along with the twelve prostitutes.

Using four longboats, the men of *Le Tiburon* made quick work of the transfer. By midnight, every one of the *Eagle* crew lay senseless on the floor of the empty sugar warehouse at the western end of the wharf, put in irons, and laid in rows. When the task was complete, Joshua called for his hundred-and-fifty men to be assembled around their captives.

"Now that we've taken the *Eagle*, fifty of you will come with Morgan and me to man her." He looked to Morgan. "As your name is called, return to *Le Tiburon*, gather your things, and begin transferring out to the *Eagle*." Joshua turned to Captain Steele. "Does that answer your question, Alan?"

"What about me? Am I to be made a slave with Mister Todd and the rest of my crew?"

"No."

"Then what are you going to do with me?"

"I'm taking you with me on the *Eagle*."

"Ah!" Captain Steele gave a nod. "You know that somebody from the *Silver Cloud* may call you for a parley, and you need me to convince them that the *Eagle* is still their protector."

"I knew you were a clever man."

"And what makes you think I would lie for you?"

"Henry!"

"Yes, Captain?" The lad stopped reading names and held up the list. "You don't want that last man?"

"The names are all good." He pointed at the unconscious men. "Choose one of Captain Steele's men and drag him over here to us."

"Aye, aye!"

Joshua turned back to Alan. "Since Henry doesn't know which of your crew you favor and which ones you don't, this will be an interesting moment."

"Here's one of the younger ones, Captain." Henry dropped the lad's arms and gave a final push with his foot. "He was the smallest and easiest to drag."

"Good choice, Henry." Joshua pulled his sword and placed the tip at the unconscious lad's chest. "You either yield and agree with my request or I run this lad through in his sleep."

"You wouldn't!"

"Oh, wouldn't I!" Joshua pressed the sword into the lad's flesh enough to draw blood. "And if his death doesn't cause you to repent, then I will kill another, and another until you do." He looked at the man for several breaths. "Your choice, Alan. This lad dies and I'll let you choose the next one—perhaps one that deserved a flogging but didn't get it yet."

"Stop! I'll cooperate!"

"I knew you didn't mean it, Alan." He turned to Henry. "You can drag the lad back where you found him." Joshua sheathed his sword, took Alan by the upper arm, and walked him away toward the warehouse doors. "I need to know your orders—what the *Silver Cloud* expects of you."

"It's simple. I'm to protect them from you."

"They named me and *Le Tiburon*?"

"Yes—among several others that might have learned about our mission."

"Who told you about me and *Le Tiburon*?" He pointed at Morgan. "Was it him?"

"No. Captain Jones told us about your attack on the *Falmouth Packet* off the coast of Georgia—that he disabled *Le Tiburon* with a lucky shot—and that you'd be out for revenge."

"An unfortunate embarrassment that will be rectified the day I kill him."

Alan looked at his unconscious crewmen. "What's going to happen to my men?"

"It's all arranged. They will be sent to a sugar cane plantation several miles inland and put to work."

"Word at the Forrestal shipyard is that you hated slavery."

"I do, but this is different."

"Call it what you may, Captain Smoot. When you force a man to work for you against his will, you have made him your slave."

"They will be released when I have the treasure."

"And that makes it different?"

"Yes—in my eyes it does." Joshua looked at the rows of sleeping men. "The moment I have the treasure, I will release you at Kings Town with the necessary papers telling the plantation to release your men."

"And what happens to them if you don't get the treasure?"

"That won't happen."

"What about me?"

"The sun will be coming up shortly." Joshua opened the warehouse door and looked east at the pinking sky. "While your men are being transported inland, you'll take Henry and me out to give us a tour of our new ship."

An hour later. Joshua and Alan climbed up the ladder and onto the deck of the privateer *Eagle* among the arriving crewmen.

"Captain?" Henry pointed across at *Le Tiburon*.

"What is it, Henry?"

"The list, Captain." He pulled the paper from his shirt. "Are you sure that Privy's the best choice to command *Le Tiburon*?"

"Well, considering the hundred men we left with him—"

"Sorry, but scuttlebutt is that it was Pritchard at the helm when that little postal packet took off your rudder a year back. In my book, that makes him—"

"Aye, it was Pritchard at the helm. He did exactly what I told him to do, and he was one of the few men who stayed with *Le Tiburon* when most of the crew left me at Savannah." Smoot gave Henry a quick glance. "Do you have a better choice?"

"Well, maybe I'm missing something, Captain, but rumor is that he's not so good in battle." Henry ran a calloused finger across his wet nose. "What if he gets into a shooting battle with the *Silver Cloud* and gets *Le Tiburon* sunk?"

"Why would you care?"

"But the crew? Those hundred men signed up for treasure just like these fifty on your list." It took Henry a moment to realize where Joshua was going. "Then…you don't care if they die, do you?"

"As I see it, Henry, if Pritchard and his men can get the treasure, then we all split it up, just like we all planned. But if they get themselves killed, that's just bigger shares for you, me, and our fifty men." Smoot ran his hands along the rail. "With this fine Virginia privateer and her new guns, we can take the *Silver Cloud* all by ourselves if we have to."

"Then…" Henry checked himself.

"The *Silver Cloud* will rightly believe that we're their protectors, Henry, and we'll play our part, just as they expect. We need the fighters from *Le Tiburon* to help get the treasure, but after that, I would be willing to help the *Silver Cloud* sink Nate Pritchard and the rest of those fish bait troublemakers."

"Troublemakers?"

"I've been watching the crew for these past two weeks, Henry. I've identified the good and the bad among them, and the list is the result." He turned to their prisoner. "I think Captain Steele would agree with me."

The older captain turned. "Agree to what?"

Joshua turned about and rested his backside against the rail. "I was only eight at the time, but I was told how Captain Rip Rap was always trading crewmen between the *King James* and the *Walrus*, and I figured the thing out."

"Oh?"

"Well, Captain Rip Rap would send all the scoundrels and cutthroats over to John Flint in exchange for the good followers—most of the ones that were pressed into service when a prize was taken. Ended up, the *Walrus* was having a mutiny most every day while the *Royal James* ran like one of the King's own men-of-war." He took the list from Henry. "That, my young friend, is how I chose the men we're taking with us on the *Eagle*."

"Now I see it."

"As soon as they get settled aboard, we'll be taking the *Eagle* for a cruise around Dead Man's Chest. That will give us a chance to see how she runs on the wind, and scout the lay of the land at the same time."

The *Eagle* was a splendid craft. She was quick at the helm and had the latest 'sharp' hull design of the privateers. Her two masts were raked aft to improve her upwind abilities, and she carried half again the sail of most other ships of equal tonnage. She was a warship from stem to stern but built along the lines of the agile racing sloops at Oxford. Her fifty new crewmen had no difficulty adjusting to her special needs.

"She's a better ship than *Le Tiburon*, Henry!" Smoot ordered her tiller to lee for the tack back to the windward side of Dead Man's Chest.

"Aye, Cap'n! She's a real fine lady all right." Joshua and Henry walked to the bow and leaned against the windward rail as the *Eagle*'s sails filled for the larboard reach back toward Christiansted. While passing the western tip of the small island, Smoot studied the line of coral and the band of white sand called Rip Rap beach.

"Do you know anything about Dead Man's Chest, Henry?"

"Only the tales about it from the old crews that stopped at Tortuga when I was just a pup."

"Then you know nothing of the reef, other than what our chart shows?"

"You've got me there, Captain." He paused. "Are you figuring the *Silver Cloud* will be putting in on the south side where the coral is split, and then anchor off Rip Rap Beach?"

"That's what I'd do if I were them, and I'd reckon that's where Captain Murray put his grandnephew ashore with the treasure."

"Does Privy know how many men to put ashore tonight?"

"It's all been arranged." Something caught Smoot's eye. At three leagues was a large merchantman with gleaming new sails on a starboard tack and paralleling Saint Croix. "Morgan!" Smoot pointed. "Is that her?

"Aye, that's her, and right on time."

"Well then, we'd best get to playing our part." Joshua turned to Captain Steele. "Forgive me for reminding you, Alan, but the lives and future of your crew depend on you convincing the *Silver Cloud* that the *Eagle* is still their protector."

CHAPTER THREE:
The Silver Cloud Arrives

Two leagues to the northwest and driven by the steady afternoon trade winds, sailed the majestic *Silver Cloud*. She was half a day ahead of schedule.

"Captain Jones!" Robert stepped close to the young captain. "I must insist you reconsider. Just because we haven't seen any pirates yet doesn't mean they aren't waiting for us on the island."

"You're being an old lady again, Robert. If our secret were out, don't you think we would know it by now?" John strode to the rail and spun on a heel with spread arms. "Where are they? Do you see any pirate ships?"

No sooner were the words out of his mouth than the foretop watch called out the familiar words. "Ship on the larboard bow!"

John shaded his eyes and searched the horizon. "It looks like the *Eagle*." John stepped to the binnacle and took up the spyglass.

David joined the two. "Is it them?"

"We'll know in a moment." John raised his spyglass and studied the ship. "I can't make out anybody on deck yet, but there's no doubt that it's the *Eagle*." John turned to the Yorkman. "Do you see, Robert? I told you our secret is safe."

"Just the same, I'll not lead anybody to the treasure until I'm certain."

"Damn it, man!" John strode to the center of the deck and pointed into the rigging. "We have lookouts in the crosstrees! Nobody can get near us without being spotted, and we have enough armament to sink a ship twice our size. If we send everybody but the gun crews, we can have the treasure dug up and back aboard within five or six hours." He waited, but Robert did not answer. "Besides, even if there were pirates about, nobody is going to attack us until we start digging."

"Just the same, it'll be my way or none."

John looked about the quarterdeck at the other officers and men on watch. Each was curious as to how the drama would play out.

John stepped close and lowered his voice. "We had best finish this discussion in my cabin." He turned to David. "Find Mister Gunn and meet us there."

David had not seen John this upset since their heated discussion about crew discipline the day they had departed Charles Town.

David found Ben in the galley helping with the noon meal. As the two made their way aft, David explained the argument between the captain and the New Yorker, and cautioned him to mind his tongue.

"I have my opinion on the matter, but I'll keep it to myself unless Captain Jones asks."

As the two entered the master's cabin, John turned to the old man "Ah, Mister Gunn. Take a seat and pour yourselves some of Scotland's finest."

John began, as if nothing was wrong. "Gentlemen, we've had a long voyage and we're very close to our goal." He reached his right hand across the green felt. "Robert, I'd like to apologize for my outburst on the quarterdeck. You're right to be cautious concerning the treasure."

"Thank you, John." Robert was surprised with John's change of mood and accepted the offered hand. "I'm acutely aware that you three, and the whole crew for that matter, are anxious to bring the treasure aboard and be on our way as quickly as possible. But I have seen how pirates work. When it comes to treachery, there's none to match them."

Ben nodded. "I can vouch for that, Master Ormerod."

John gave the old man a paternal smile and turned back to Robert. "You claim that you had a plan, Robert. Now's the time to tell us, before we get to our anchorage."

"As I was saying on deck, we can't be too careful. If there are pirates about, they most likely already have a contingent on the island waiting for us. The moment they see us begin digging for the treasure, they'll attack."

While Robert explained the details of his plan, Ben Gunn turned the chart about on the table. "Beggin' yer pardon, Captain Jones, but where do you plan on leavin' the ship while we're ashore?"

"We'll drop anchor at this opening in the reef." John pointed with his dagger and looked to Robert for confirmation. "Isn't that where you told us your granduncle put the *Royal James* when he put you ashore?"

Robert nodded. "Yes, right there."

"While we're ashore, Captain, who's to watch the ship?"

"Good question, David." John touched the map. "We'll be leaving Captain Van Mourik and the cannon crews aboard. The winds will swing the ship about to expose her starboard cannons to seaward. Between our long guns and the *Eagle* patrolling the deep waters outside the reef, no ship would risk an approach."

"Then Ben and I will go ashore with you and Mister Ormerod?"

"Of course."

By dusk, the *Silver Cloud* had come within three hundred yards of their protector and traded both semaphore and hand waves with the *Eagle*. Captain Jones and Captain Steele studied each other through their spyglasses for nearly a minute before the larger ship finally dropped anchor just outside the island's protective reef. As expected, the winds pushed the camouflaged frigate about its anchor into the perfect position to give any approaching vessel a full broadside.

As the sun set beyond the port of Christiansted five miles to the southwest, final preparations were underway for the morning's assault on Dead Man's Chest.

The southern two-thirds of Dead Man's Chest was dominated by a ridgeline that reached several hundred feet while the northern third was a rolling plain covered with waist-high grass and an occasional bush that reached to a man's shoulders. A half-mile north from Rip Rap Beach stood Dorsal Rock, a hump of black volcanic stone fifty feet long, twenty feet wide, and a dozen feet high. It was so named because it resembled the back of a dolphin breaking the surface for a breath of air. It was an excellent spot to bury a treasure. Ten minutes at a quick pace brought the shore party to its western end.

John stopped and turned about to survey the surrounding land. "This is it?"

"There's none better." Robert pointed at the hill to the south. "There were only four of us, and we had to find a place close to the beach to carry the bags, chests, and boxes." He pointed at the line of trees a hundred yards away. "This is far enough from cover that we couldn't be watched and attacked. A compromise to be sure, but weighing all the dangers we were faced with, it was the most logical choice."

John pointed back the way they had come. "But your granduncle put you ashore back on the west beach." He turned and pointed to the nearby north shore. "Why didn't he set you ashore here, closer to this spot?"

"He was already gone when I decided this was the best place."

"But—"

"He left us a single ship's boat, so we used it to float the treasure around the point to this north beach."

"Well, Robert." John spread his arms. "We're waiting for you. Please."

With a nod, Robert walked away to the eastern end of the mound. After what seemed to be an endless contemplation, he strode off to the south for ten paces, stopped and turned ninety degrees to the right. At the fourth step, he stopped and drove his sword into the fertile topsoil. He turned and called back. "Here! This is where we dig!"

The Indian fighters smelled it first—that unmistakable acrid odor of unclean men. By ones and twos, they turned toward the nearby hill to the east.

David noticed the men's concern and whispered to John. "Something's wrong, John. Look at our fighters." By now, all the men had dropped their digging tools and taken defensive positions.

"Aye, Robert!" John pointed south. "Look there—to the tree line!"

There was a flash of reflected sunlight, followed by several others.

"I knew it." Robert stepped to John and pulled his pistols from his sash. "Exactly as I feared."

John climbed up the side of the rock. "Listen up!" He pointed. "We've a large group of men hiding at the tree line several hundred yards to the southeast! Now that the treasure's location has been revealed…"

It was too late for making plans, for out of the trees and through the tall grass came thirty hairy sea dogs, running at top speed and screaming like men just released from hell. Each carried a cutlass and a brace of pistols slung about his shoulder. A hundred yards from the mound, the pirates broke into four separate groups and continued their charge directly toward Robert's planted sword.

When the pirates were at fifty yards, John barked his command. "Fire!"

☠ ☠ ☠

The *Silver Cloud* had been left with a skeleton crew—just enough men to man the long chase guns should an enemy ship approach. She was anchored three hundred yards beyond the reef, giving her plenty of room to swing about her chain. If all went as planned ashore, she would be back to the safety of deep water by late afternoon of that same day, and the treasure would be safe within her lazarette.

The sun was still low on the morning horizon when the battle began on the north shore. From the *Silver Cloud*, the sound of the pistol fire could easily have been mistaken for the popping of green wood in the galley stove, but the cook was ashore and his fires were cold. Jack Van Mourik and most of the gunners lay peacefully asleep in their hammocks about the deck. Only two of their mates remained awake, pacing quietly about the quarterdeck and forecastle.

It was the forward watch who heard the pistol fire first. Within minutes of his call, all hands except the old Dutchman were climbing into the rigging. If they were lucky, they hoped to catch a glimpse of the battle from the upper yards. Within minutes, all hands were perched in the crosstrees—except for one man.

It was the Savannah carpenter's mate—Joshua Smoot's man—who had signed onto the *Silver Cloud* a week before sailing. There were objections to this hasty replacement for the man killed in a freak accident, but he had good references and the position was critical to the mission.

If the rest of the crew had been sharp, they would have noticed that while they climbed as high as possible into the rigging, this young carpenter's mate climbed only a short way up—not nearly high enough to see over the island's low ridge to the grassy flats of the north shore and Dorsal Rock.

With their attention thus diverted by the gunfire, the gunners failed to notice when Joshua Smoot's saboteur dropped to the deck.

He looked aft. "Ha! Van Mourik is still asleep!" With another quick glance into the rigging to make certain that his absence and strange actions had gone unnoticed, he ran forward with the swiftness of a cat and lowered a bucket into the jade-green waters. He then wet the deck from gunwale to anchor cable in an irregular pattern of splashes and footprints, then dried his feet, and replaced the bucket and rags at their station.

With another quick glance upward, he pulled loose the cable's wraps about the bitt and then cut the stopper. Nothing moved. It would not take much of a breeze to set the great ship in motion. And then, once the cable began its run across the deck, nothing could stop it.

Before the ship gave its first lurch, the traitor was once again high in the rigging, balanced atop the main top gallant yard next to the same gunner's mate who had given him a hand up earlier.

The breeze from the southeast had now freshened to five knots—more than enough to pull the great anchor chain from the ship. Several of the men in the uppermost rigging noticed the movement, but none—save the saboteur—realized what had happened until it was too late. As her keel ground to a stop on the line of submerged coral, the great vessel shuddered, throwing one of the seamen from a yardarm to the sea far below.

The gunner's mate standing on the yard next to the traitor looked about and cried out. "What was that?"

"Look!" The traitor pointed down at the bow with feigned dismay. "The anchor chain's gone and we're on the reef!"

As quickly as they could, all thirty-one of the sailors slid the sheets to the deck.

"Vat is dat?" Captain Van Mourik jumped up from his slumber, stumbled about the deck for a moment, and rubbed his swollen face. He gazed about the deck, trying to remember where he was.

"We're in trouble, Dutch!" McCoy was the senior gunner and did not respect the overweight Dutchman enough to address him by his proper title.

"Trouble? What trouble?"

"Look!" McCoy ran forward to the wet footprints. "Someone came aboard and released our anchor chain, and we've drifted onto the coral!"

Without waiting for Van Mourik to remember his instructions from Captain Jones, McCoy gave the order to fire three cannons.

☠ ☠ ☠

David studied the apparent confusion among the attacking pirates. "What on earth are they doing?"

"I see it, David. It's as if they've never been in battle before, or they've no leader."

"Look!" Robert pointed at one group of pirates that were especially confused. "I say that their problem is that they've too many leaders." He looked to John and received the expected nod.

Each group consisted of seven to nine men and seemed confused about which way to go, or which tactic to use next. Visible in-fighting broke out at the pirate's right flank, first with shouts of disagreement, and then with a discharged flintlock. Within minutes, their main force had moved forward far enough that the little group of bickering pirates was now completely isolated from the rest. Before they could figure out what had gone wrong, two of their number were cut down by rifle balls, leaving seven. Three of these dropped their weapons and fled back toward the tree line. One of the remaining four ran toward the main body of pirates while the other three turned and ran toward the water in a desperate attempt to avoid the thick rifle fire from John's battle-seasoned Indian fighters. These three fell dead on the sand just short of the sea.

John and Robert climbed to the top of the rock for a better view of the battlefield. Following John's hand signals, David and four of the Indian fighters circled along the pirate's left flank while the Bosun and his men took the other flank. At every ten paces, David and the Bosun turned to watch for John's signal. While David turned to proceed, one of the fleeing pirates from the aborted attack ran headlong into David, knocking the young Jamaican flat on his back.

"Mercy!" The young man of no more than twenty, was too startled to do anything but cry out. "Mercy! I surrender!"

A pirate called out in panic. "They be all about us, mates!" He jumped up and fired both of his pistols at David's men with no effect. The rest of the men stood and began firing in panic before breaking and running back for the tree line. When the last flintlock was fired and the final sword was wiped clean of dishonest blood, eighteen of the thirty pirates lay dead or dying on the north plain of Dead Man's Chest.

"Bosun!" Captain Jones followed Robert down to the ground. "Sound the order to reassemble!"

"Aye, aye, Cap'n!" Within ten minutes, all the bodies had been found and dragged to the beach for viewing. John stepped among them. "We should have taken one captive so we could interrogate him."

"I have one!" David pushed the young pirate forward. "This one has already agreed to talk."

"Good!" John pointed to the rock. "Bring him here!"

"John." Robert looked to the sword that was still planted in the ground. "A word!"

"Yes?"

Robert leaned close and whispered. "Before we begin questioning that young man, there's something I must tell you."

John gave a huff. "What now?"

Robert walked to his sword and put a hand on the hilt. "The treasure isn't here."

"What?" Everyone within earshot turned and looked at the two. "What do you mean, the treasure isn't here?"

"It's on the island John, but not here where I planted my sword."

"You risked the lives of my crew for..." John paused, suddenly realizing what Robert had done. He whispered. "You knew we'd be attacked, didn't you?"

"I was almost certain of it, and I didn't want the treasure's location revealed to those scoundrels—whomever they are."

"Couldn't you have told us, or at least me?"

Robert nodded. "Of course, I could have, but if the men knew they were defending empty dirt instead of the treasure, do you suppose for a moment they would have fought quite so gallantly?"

John turned and looked at the dead. Only one of the *Silver Cloud*'s crew had been killed. "No, I suppose not."

"May I assume then, that you're not angry with me?"

"No, I'm not angry with you, Robert. I would ask, however, that from now on, you be honest with me."

"As you wish, John." He turned back toward the captive pirate. "Shall we see what our prisoner has to tell us?"

While John and Robert began their interrogation of the prisoner, David climbed to the top of Dorsal Rock and spotted a ship to the east and silhouetted against the morning sun. He turned and called. "Captain Jones!" Before he could finish, the *Silver Cloud*'s three cannon reports reached the north shore.

"Something's happened!" John turned and looked south.

"It's the *Eagle*!" David pointed to the northeast. "Captain Steele is supposed to be protecting the *Silver Cloud*!"

"I told Van Mourik to fire three cannons if there was trouble." He looked north to their protector. "As for the *Eagle*, I must assume Captain Steele heard the battle and figured we needed help." John made a quick survey of his men and turned to Robert. "I want you to remain here with six of the Indian fighters to protect our wounded and get what you can from that prisoner." He looked about at the others. "The rest of you will come with me!"

"Do you think the *Silver Cloud* is under attack?"

"They can't be under attack, David, or there'd be more cannon fire."

John spun and looked to the *Eagle* once more. "The man may hate me, but Alan Steele would never abandon the *Silver Cloud* if there were an enemy within sight."

After ten minutes of running, John and his men rounded the last row of trees, giving them a clear view of their ship's upper rigging.

David ran at John's side. "Can you tell what's wrong?"

"It's hard to say for certain, but I believe the ship's listing slightly." A moment later, the two came to a stop on Rip Rap Beach. What met their gaze confused them greatly. There was now no doubt that the *Silver Cloud* was on the reef, but they were more puzzled by the strange activity at her waterline.

"This is all I need!" John pulled his sword from the sheath. "A mutiny!"

☠ ☠ ☠

McCoy was beginning to lower the first of two cannons over the side and into the bow of a waiting ship's boat when the shore party arrived back at Rip Rap Beach. The small craft sank nearly to her gunwales as the heavy cannon settled amongst the powder kegs, tools, and various shot loads.

While McCoy shoved off toward shore, John and his first officer stopped at the water's edge, with Ben Gunn tottering far behind.

"What on earth?" David stopped next to John. "Is that even our crew?"

"Oh, there's no doubt about that!" John could point out the various men by name. "That's McCoy at the first boat's helm." John studied the ship carefully. "The question you should be asking is why they've turned against us."

Ben finally caught up. "What's happening, Cap'n?"

"See for yourself, Ben." John pointed to the slow-moving boats at the *Cloud*'s water line. "While we were fighting pirates on the north shore, our loyal gunners decided to put the *Silver Cloud* on the reef and steal two cannons."

"Steal our cannons?" Ben struggled for his breath. "That doesn't make no sense, Cap'n. That isn't how you steal cannons."

As the old maroon watched, John and David chose several of the men and launched one of the boats. John pulled his two pistols and turned back to Ben. "Are you coming with us?"

"No, Cap'n! I'll wait here with the others. There's sure to be gunfire, an' I'd just be in the way."

Midway between the crippled *Silver Cloud* and Rip Rap Beach, eight flint-lock pistols leveled on the five gunners who were pulling toward the beach in the first boat.

"Heave to, Mister McCoy, and explain this mutiny!"

"Mutineers, you call us?" The startled gunner ordered his men to ship oars and then threw the tiller to starboard to stop his boat. "Are you daft, Captain Jones?"

"No, I'm not! Unless you have a good explanation for these bizarre actions, your life will be forfeited here and now!"

"Captain, you mistake us!" It was one of the other gunners. "We're not traitors!"

"Then why is my ship laying on the reef with a dozen of my gunners stealing two of my cannons?" John swung his pistol arm about and pointed toward the beach. "Were you planning on cutting us down with grapeshot as we returned with the treasure?"

"Captain Jones!" McCoy stood. "Before you make a complete jackass of yourself, Captain Jones, you'd best hear what happened while you were gone!"

"I'm listening!"

"Someone came aboard from the sea during all that shooting across the island and released our anchor chain. None of us saw him because we were watching your battle."

David called to the man. "And how do you know it wasn't one of your own men?"

"The deck was still wet where he came over the rail. By the time the chain finally began slipping from the hawsepipe, the man was back in the sea and long gone."

John lowered his pistols and gestured for his men to do the same. "What about these two cannons and all that ammunition?" Four casks of powder and a score of balls lay in each boat's bottom, along with the other equipment necessary to carry on a protracted land battle.

"That's how I explain it, Captain Jones!" McCoy stood and pointed seaward, past the *Silver Cloud*, to the ship approaching from the southeast. "By the time that ship gets here, our ship will have listed too far larboard to use her seaward guns!" McCoy pointed to the northwest. "Without the *Eagle* to protect us…" McCoy gritted his teeth and looked back at the fat Dutchman watching from the ship. That stupid Dutchman…" He turned back to his captain. "I had to make a decision!"

John made a quick survey of the approaching ship. "Take a look at her, David. Is that who I think it is?"

David pulled his spyglass from its pouch and raised it to his eye. "Good Lord! It's *Le Tiburon*! That's Joshua Smoot!"

"I thought so."

McCoy looked to the approaching ship. "Do you know her?"

John turned back to his gunner. "Winter of last year, Mister Noble and I were attacked by that ship several leagues south of Savannah. Before her crew could board us, Lady Luck helped us to tear her rudder off with one shot of bar stock." John suddenly realized why McCoy was taking the two cannons ashore. He glanced quickly at the island and at the approaching pirate ship. He pointed to the island. "McCoy, get those cannons ashore and up to that cliff! We're in for another battle!"

David pushed the rudder over to turn their boat around. "They must think we already have the treasure."

John gave a nod and reached out for David's spyglass. "No doubt about it. Our gunfire on the north shore was obviously the signal to release our anchor, and the Cloud's three cannons signaled Smoot to begin his attack." John paused. "I wish there was some way for them to find out we haven't dug up the treasure yet."

David straightened the tiller and paralleled the two boats with the cannons. "Why don't we release the prisoners?"

"Why should I do that?"

"Because they know we don't have the treasure, and they might signal Smoot to break off his attack."

"You're right!" John turned toward the beach and called out. "Mister Gunn!"

The old man called back. "I was right, wasn't I? They weren't stealin' 'em after all!"

"Send one of the men back to the north shore to tell Mister Ormerod to release the uninjured prisoners!"

"Aye, aye, Cap'n!"

"Make sure he tells the prisoners that the treasure wasn't at Dorsal Rock!" He turned back to David. "Good thinking, David."

David pointed to the northeast, back past Rip Rap Beach. "Look! It's the *Eagle*, and they've come about! Maybe they can get back around the reef before *Le Tiburon* gets close enough to attack!"

"Not likely with these winds. I'm afraid our only real hope is to get these cannons into position before Smoot gets within range." John looked back toward the *Silver Cloud* and called to McCoy. "I trust the remaining gunners know to move all the swivel guns to the starboard gunwale."

McCoy called back. "Aye, Captain! My boys know their jobs!"

Pulling the 800-pound cannons through the sand and up the hill to the cliff took just over an hour and all the available men. The small wooden wheels were designed for the hard planking of a ship's deck, and fortunately, McCoy brought enough spare planking to lay down on the soft sand. Using a combination of dead heads buried along the way and the blocks and tackle the gunners had brought along, they made quicker progress than expected. They finally twisted the second cannon about to face down toward their stricken ship just as *Le Tiburon* set up for her first attack run.

David watched the pirate ship through his spyglass. "*Le Tiburon* is within range of the Cloud, Captain Jones. What are they waiting for?"

"With the cannons hidden as they are, Smoot must think she's unarmed. He's going to get close before he fires on her."

The words had no more left his mouth than two of *Le Tiburon*'s cannons fired, sending splashes just short of the stricken ship. John put a hand on McCoy's shoulder. "Steady now, McCoy, and make this count."

Aye, Captain." The gunner sighted down his barrel at the approaching ship. "On your command, sir."

"Fire!"

CHAPTER FOUR:
Dead Man's Chest

*T*he *Silver Cloud's* distress signal rolled like thunder across the sea in all directions, bringing Henry Morgan down the *Eagle's* companionway to his captain's door. He gave two taps with the hilt of his cutlass and stepped back. "Captain Smoot! Did ya hear it?"

Joshua had just begun a breakfast of biscuits and gravy with Captain Steele. "Excuse me." He wiped his face clean, stepped across, and pulled open the cabin door. "Of course, I heard it, Henry. That's why we're here on the north side of the island."

"Then…" Henry paused in thought. "This must mean Privy's men got the treasure and *Le Tiburon* has attacked the *Silver Cloud.*"

Smoot paused to listen for additional cannon shots. "You're wrong, Henry! Those three cannon shots were a warning signal, not a battle. I'd say they just now lost their anchor and went up on the reef."

"But—"

"Go!" Smoot pointed. "We've been gone long enough. Come about and head for the south shore."

"Aye, Captain."

Smoot turned to rejoin his breakfast guest. "A busy morning, isn't it Alan?"

"Aye, and as much as I know I should not be telling you this, Captain Jones is going to want an explanation for why I abandoned the *Silver Cloud.*"

"Hmm." Joshua thought for a moment. "What were your orders?"

"First, if a ship approaches, position the *Eagle* between it and the *Silver Cloud.*"

"Anything else?"

"When I am certain the *Silver Cloud* is safe, I'm to make a circuit of the island to make sure there are no other ships."

"Well then, we'll wait and see if he asks."

Before the *Eagle* had reached the western tip of Dead Man's Chest, *Le Tiburon* was positioning herself for her first broadside, seemingly unconcerned by the occasional small iron balls flying through her rigging. At one hundred yards abeam, she backed all but her fore top gallant for steerage, and coasted to a near halt in the calm sea. Expecting little if any opposition, Captain Pritchard brought his twenty-two-gun ship as close to the coral as was safe, putting it well within the range of the yet-unseen shore battery atop the hill.

"Gunners!" Pritchard studied the *Silver Cloud*'s siding. "They be unarmed, mates, so take yer time strippin' off her plankin'!" At Pritchard's order, two cannons threw their twenty-pound balls at the *Silver Cloud*'s exposed underbelly. Neither shot found its mark, and before the deafening roar of *Le Tiburon*'s cannons spent themselves to the horizon, there were two similar explosions on the cliff above and to the right of Rip Rap Beach.

Pritchard and half his crew saw the white puffs of smoke. "What the—?" Before he could finish his oath, the first of McCoy's two rounds smashed into the bulwarks just above *Le Tiburon*'s number-three starboard cannon, killing two men instantly and sending a shower of oak splinters across the gun deck. The second ball followed the first by five seconds, hitting the mizzen topmast a glancing blow, tearing away several inches of wood just above the crosstrees.

"What the hell?"

"There!" One of his gunners pointing. "They got cannons on that cliff!"

By the time Pritchard had taken up the spyglass, McCoy and his gun crews had reloaded and fired again at *Le Tiburon*. This third shot struck the pirate ship's hull just above the waterline amidships, punching a three-foot hole in the planking.

"Come about!" As the great ship began its turn to larboard, Pritchard turned back to the gun crews. "Fire as you bear!" One by one, and then in twos and threes, the eleven cannons began firing on the *Silver Cloud*. But since the ship was well into her turn, only the first three shots came close to their marks. While the shore battery reloaded for their next volley, the gunners aboard the *Silver Cloud* continued peppering *Le Tiburon* with small balls from their pistols and larger balls from the eight swivel guns. Two of the one-inch balls found their mark, killing one pirate and wounding a second man.

Smoot watched the whole affair through his spyglass. "Morgan! Trim your sails for more speed and if we get within range, begin firing on *Le Tiburon*!"

"At *Le Tiburon*?" Henry was confused. "Don't you mean the *Silver Cloud*?"

"No!" Smoot lowered his spyglass. "Not until we know for sure that treasure is found!"

"But we do!" Henry pointed back toward the north shore. "Privy's men attacked them when they started digging!"

"Only when I see the chests of gold and silver with my own eyes, will I be convinced. Until then, we've no choice but to play the *Silver Cloud*'s protector, just like they expect us to do."

Before *Le Tiburon* had sailed beyond range, she had put two holes in the *Cloud* while taking seven hits herself from the shore battery. She had a small fire burning in the forecastle, and nearly a dozen of her crew lay dead or injured. By the time the *Eagle* began throwing balls at her, *Le Tiburon* had finished her turn and was running toward the safety of Cotton Garden Point near the eastern tip of Saint Croix.

"McCoy!" John stood on the ledge thirty feet above the cannons. "I want you and the other six gunners to remain here while I go meet with David and Ben when they return. If you see *Le Tiburon* turn back for another attack, fire at will."

John trotted down the dusty path to the beach. David and Ben Gunn had just climbed down into one of the ship's boats and were now pulling toward the beach.

As soon as they were within earshot, John called out. "Did they hit her?"

David called back. "Three hits, Captain!"

"How bad is it?"

"Only two of their three shots penetrated the hull!" The boat skidded onto the sand and David leaped out. "One close to the bow and the second one amidships!"

"How long do you think it'll take for repairs?"

"The one at the bow is high enough that we can leave it alone until we're underway." David touched his side. "The other one is just below the waterline amidship and is pretty large. I'd say repairs will take a full day, provided the pirates leave us alone long enough to get her off the reef, moved to the beach, and hauled down."

"Smoot will be more than busy with his own repairs." John looked out to the fleeing pirates. "They're on fire and I believe we damaged one of their masts."

"Good!" David pointed at the *Eagle* as it continued to pursue *Le Tiburon*. "Between our shore battery and Captain Steele, we should be well protected."

John watched the *Eagle* for several moments. "I misjudged Captain Steele."

☠ ☠ ☠

While the tide receded, John, David, and Ben stood watching their injured ship list further and further toward shore, Robert trotted onto the north end of the beach with several Indian fighters.

"Is it bad, John?"

"Aye!" John called back. "Bad enough! David and Ben tell me that there's a large hole amidships at the waterline." John took several steps toward Robert and stopped. "How did it go with the prisoner? Did you get my message?"

"It's done, just as you ordered."

"Did he believe you—that the treasure wasn't there?"

Robert nodded. "I made him watch while we dug a hole where I had planted my sword. He promised to signal his that the treasure was not there if we'd let them go."

"Good." John stepped into the boat. "I'm going out to see the damage myself. While I'm gone, David, make sure the gun crews on the cliff are provided with food, water, and some shelter from the sun. It's going to be a long day." He turned to Robert. "Would you and Mister Gunn accompany me?"

Within a half-hour, John, Robert, Ben, and Captain Van Mourik were inside the crippled ship's lower decks inspecting the damage. It was now low tide, and the ship was listing nearly fifteen degrees from the upright. The hole in her side was now two spans above the sea.

"That looks bad." John pulled away several loose pieces of oak from the large breach.

"As I tolt Master Noble, we took three rounds to de hull, Cap'n, an' there's some damage to her innards besides." Van Mourik spread a sheet of parchment on the deck and pointed to the areas of greatest damage.

"Damage to the innards?" John looked at the drawing. "How much? Where?"

"Here and here." Van Mourik pointed to a lower-deck beam and stanchion. "I tolt David we can leave der hole in the bow alone, but we'll have to move her to Rip Rap Beach at de next tide ta fix dis one, ja?"

"Can you have your temporary patches in place that quickly?"

"Aye, an' she be ready to float clear of da reef by den."

By late afternoon, the hole at the *Silver Cloud*'s waterline was covered with a temporary patch of canvas and tar, and by sunset, just as the Dutchman had predicted, the sea had returned far enough that three of the boats were able to pull the great ship free from the coral and into the deeper waters. By dusk the *Silver Cloud* was secured near the high-water mark of Rip Rap Beach. The heaving-down post had been buried deep in the sand and a winching system put in place long before the ship had reached the shore.

A heavy line was attached to the mainmast crosstree and run several times through a block and tackle system attached to the post. While the heavy ship was hauled down to expose its damaged hull to the carpenters, John met with his officers.

"The carpenter tells me that if there are no more attacks by the pirates, the permanent repairs could be completed in two days." He poured himself a cup of tea and looked back at his crippled ship. Lanterns were being set up to give the carpenters the light they needed to begin the removal of the damaged sections of planking.

"We figured as much." Robert mixed a spoon of sugar in his cup. "Was that the something important you wanted to tell us?"

"No, it wasn't." John gave the older man a raise of his brows. "Today's encounter with pirates—both on the north shore and from the sea—has put this mission into a completely different light and forced an important decision upon us."

Robert was suddenly suspicious. "What kind of decision?"

"You could have been killed this morning."

Robert looked at the others. "Any one of us could have been killed."

"But you're still the only one who knows where the treasure is buried. If you are killed, we won't get the treasure, and General Washington won't get his cannons."

"I'm aware of that risk, John, but Mister Jefferson gave me explicit orders to tell nobody, including you, until we have our shovels in hand."

"He didn't even trust me?"

"That's why he didn't ask me for a map." Robert took a sip of his tea. "Once it was put to paper, anybody who managed to get their hands on it could get the treasure."

Ben stepped close. "Beggin' yer pardon, sir, but Captain Jones is right. It doesn't matter anymore what Mister Jefferson told you. You have to tell the rest of us."

Robert considered the old man's admonition.

David knew he was the youngest among them, but he felt compelled to be a part of the debate. "You shouldn't have to ponder this, Mister Ormerod. You know Ben and John are right. You have to tell us where it's buried."

Robert considered for a long moment. He gave a huff and stepped to the table where the map tubes lay. "Which one of these contains the chart of the island?"

"Here it is." John pulled the chart from the tube and spread it across the table, weighing it down with a lamp at each end.

The chart showed the outline of the island with the reef and beach at the west end, but none of the island's interior detail. Robert dipped a quill in John's ink well and drew a heavy meandering line across the island from the east toward the western end. Then, near the center of this first line, he drew a second one, perpendicular to the first and running halfway toward the northern shore.

"It's here." Robert touched the spot with his finger rather than make a mark with the quill. "Right at the head of this valley. We figured the trees and bushes would grow the best there."

John looked at the spot. "Can you be more specific?"

"Yes, I can. As you are climbing the hill, you will come to the point where this valley disappears into the ridgeline. Twenty paces back down into the valley you will come to a manchineel tree." Robert looked up at his three friends. "The treasure lies under its roots."

David touched John's arm. "When do we go, Captain?"

John looked across at his ship. "If we bring the treasure down before the ship's ready to sail, we'll have pirates on us like lice on a maroon."

Ben chased an itch across his chest and up the side of his neck. "They'll be all over us no matter when we dig it up, Cap'n. Why wait?"

"Aye." John held up a hand and looked at Robert. "I have an idea."

"Oh?"

"Since we already know they'll be watching our every move, why not turn it to our advantage?"

"What kind of advantage, John?"

"You've all heard the fable about the little boy who cried wolf." He looked about at the men one at a time. They each nodded. "Why did the townsfolk stop coming to the boy's aid?"

"Because he called for help three or four times when there was no wolf." David looked to John. "The false alarms caused the people to stop believing the boy."

"We're going to cry treasure to the pirates?"

"Yes, Robert."

"How?"

John lifted one of the lamps and let the map roll closed. "I intend to send out two or three digging parties a day with empty wooden boxes. The men will be instructed to select an obvious spot in the trees or along the coast and dig a hole. Then, after they bury their boxes, they will return to Rip Rap Beach. Another team of a dozen or so men will go out and dig those same boxes up and bring them back to the beach."

Ben scratched his throat and squinted through his confusion. "I may be a little slow, Cap'n, but where's the sense in that?"

"I understand." Robert turned to the old man. "After a dozen or so false holes, the pirates will tire of watching. When we finally send out the real treasure hunters, the pirates won't be able to tell the real from the false."

"Exactly." John was pleased. "Another benefit is that it will keep those who aren't repairing the ship busy."

Robert raised a hand. "You told us that there was something else we should do."

"One of us can pay a visit to Captain Steele to let him know what's going on." John turned to David. "That will be your job."

"But shouldn't you go? You're the captain."

"Aye, but Captain Steele and I have some bad history. I doubt the man would allow me aboard."

"When do you want me to go?"

"Tomorrow morning, just after breakfast. We can send out a couple of shovel crews before dark, and more early in the morning while you are at the *Eagle*. I'd like to hear Captain Steele's reaction to it our little game."

"And what if I run into trouble aboard the *Eagle*? What signal should I give you?"

"Trouble?" John raised his hands. "What kind of trouble could you get into?"

"There's pirates afoot, Captain. They could be anywhere."

John laughed and looked at the others. "Fine. If you get to the *Eagle* and discover that the whole crew has been replaced by pirates, wave your handkerchief in the air."

The others joined John in a hearty laugh.

David looked about at the other three. "My kerchief is bright yellow."

CHAPTER FIVE:
The Battle at Dorsal Rock

A dozen sleeping tents had been erected along a single line running north to south, just above the high-water mark. Armed watches stood near the end tents, and two others stood watch aboard the hauled-down ship, one at the bow and the other at the stern. Further up the beach, almost to the tree line, an extra sail was held aloft by upright oars and stretched taut to create a shaded work pavilion for the officers. Similar pavilions were erected next to the ship and circled with oil lamps so the carpenters could work throughout the night at fitting the fresh planking to the *Silver Cloud*'s hull.

It was just after midnight. Neither John nor Robert had been able to sleep. Somewhere aboard the *Silver Cloud*, a lone sailor sang a familiar verse from a sea ballad to the accompaniment of his concertina.

"A curse on the jewels, the pearls an' the gold,

A curse on the pirates, what's honor was sold.

A curse on the Yorkman, what refuses to tell,

Of the treasure laid by — may he rot in hell."

Robert swung his legs out of his cot, stood, and walked across to the small cast iron stove. He picked up the teapot, shook it to judge its contents, and took a sip of the strong brew.

John looked across the pavilion at Robert. "He's singing about you, isn't he?"

"Yes, I am the Yorkman of song and fable." Robert looked about the camp. Everything was quiet except for the sounds of the carpenters from the far side of the ship. "But the way things have gone so far, I've a bad feeling the whole crew may taste of that curse before we get off this island."

John got up and poured himself a cup. "You made the right decision to tell us."

Robert did not answer. His mind was on the treasure. The secret had been his for over twenty years, and it had given him a sort of power. A large secret will do that, especially when it concerns money. It also gave him a tremendous sense of security, knowing that any time he needed it, he could sail to this—his private island bank—and take away what he needed.

"What is it, Robert? You look a hundred leagues away."

"Oh, I was just thinking." He downed his tea and threw the last quarter inch of liquid and wilted leaves onto the dark sand. "Remember the other day when I asked you how you learned that the treasure was so large?"

"Yes?"

"I don't mean anything personal against the lad, but doesn't it strike you as a little odd that it was David who told you?"

"Who else, if not David?"

"Look at it, John. His father owns the cannons, and David knew all about me and the treasure, but he waited to tell you until you were desperate."

"Do you think David was being controlled by his father and John Silver?"

"Yes." Robert nodded. "I'd like a talk with David, provided you have no objections. I have a distinct feeling that he isn't telling us everything he knows." Robert fell silent in answer to John's raised hand. "What is it, John?"

"Listen!" The young captain bristled like a threatened dog. "Something's wrong." John stood and looked across the camp to the north. A group of men had assembled and were speaking in agitated tones.

"There!" Robert pointed. "Someone's running this way!"

While they watched, a powder monkey named Gilcrest ran down the line of tents, under the Cloud's masts and haul-down tackle, and then straight for the pavilion.

John called to the boy. "What's wrong, Gilcrest? What has happened?"

The lad was still thirty yards out when he started crying something about a man missing. But then, just before reaching them, the boy fell face down into the sand.

Robert ran out and jerked the boy up. "Who's been taken, lad?"

"The pirates took him, sir!" Gilcrest pointed back toward the north. "They took the old man—Ben Gunn!"

One of the Indian fighters ran to them and pointed to the north. "On the beach, north of Dorsal Rock!"

"Damn!" John buttoned up his breeches, strapped on his sword, and jammed two pistols into his belt.

After a few words with Robert, John and David led the rescue party northward out of camp. With their lanterns trimmed to a flicker, the darkness quickly swallowed them from sight.

As they neared Dorsal Rock, David whispered to John. "I know this is probably stupid of me to say, but aren't we walking into an ambush?"

"Aye." John stopped on the south side of the rock and turned back to the others. "Listen up. We're being watched by the men we didn't kill this morning." He pointed to the smoldering fire. "They set that fire out there to lure us into the open where they can fire on us, so I want you to pair up with a mate and follow Mister Noble and me by twos. Until I give the order, I do not want any of you to break ranks, regardless of what you see or hear. Is that understood?" There was a muffled response and nodding heads. "If we're attacked, everyone is to return to this spot and use your pistols to best advantage, being sure to watch your flanks."

The nearest crewman nodded and began passing the word.

"Then let's get to it!"

Like a flood of ants at a picnic lunch, the rescue party poured around the eastern end of the rock and north to the high-water line. Then they turned eastward toward the darkened campfire where they hoped to find their old shipmate alive.

"Please—no more!" The cry was faint, but it was the voice of Ben Gunn. John quickened his pace. One of the two fires had already died for lack of fuel, and the other was reduced to a bed of coals that sent up occasional flurries of sparks.

David reached the fires first.

"He's here, Captain! Hurry!" Ben was stripped naked and lay on his face, with a small puddle of blood in the sand where it had run from his mouth and nose. The smell of burnt flesh hung heavy over the old man.

"Is he alive?" John stepped to the old man.

"Yes but barely." David pointed. "Look at his legs, John." David pulled a cauterizing iron from the coals. "They burned him with this."

"Aye." John rolled Ben onto this back. "Ben! Can you hear me?" While he tried to revive the old man, there was a clatter of oars being shipped and of boats skidding onto the sand, announcing the arrival of Robert Ormerod and the extra men.

John turned and called. "Robert! Is that you?"

"Yes!" The Yorkman ran across to the rescue party. "Is he alive?"

"He is, but they've tortured him."

Robert dropped to his knees. "Ben!" He turned his old friend onto his back. "Ben, can you hear me?"

"Oh God...my legs are..." The old maroon whispered through bloody teeth. "I didn't...oh...Robert...they kept burning me..."

"Save your strength, Ben." Robert cradled his friend's head in his hands and looked down at his legs. Both calves were branded with a line of triangle burns from his ankles to his knees. The old man closed his eyes and swooned back into oblivion.

John stood and pointed back where Robert had come ashore. "Robert, put Ben in one of your boats and take him back to our camp as quickly as you can. He needs the doctor's care, and I'm afraid he wouldn't survive the damage it would inflict on him if we tried to carry him that far."

"You're not coming with us?" Robert looked at the men who had set a perimeter. "We came with only three men in each boat. We've plenty of room for you."

"Not just yet." John pointed at the row of nine bodies that were laid out on the other side of the fire. "What do you make of that?"

Robert turned and looked about at the dead. "Aren't those some of the men we killed here during that battle?"

"Yes, but we didn't lay them in a row like that."

"Well, that doesn't make any more sense than Joshua Smoot torturing his old friend."

"Old friend?" John gave a questioning tilt of his head. "The way I heard it, Ben was there when John Flint kidnapped Joshua and killed his mother." John shook his head. "I think Smoot must have figured that as close as you and Ben have been for all this time that you've shared the location of the treasure with him."

"No. Ben told me all about that day in Savannah, and how he was the only person on the *Walrus* that protected Joshua. Joshua Smoot would never hurt his old friend like this." He looked toward the trees. "Those men that attacked us at Dorsal Rock must be another crew of pirates that got word about our mission and got here ahead of us."

"That makes sense." John looked back at the rock and down at the two. "Since Smoot would want the treasure for himself, he would want to kill off all competitors as much as we would." John knelt down. "First things first. Let's get Ben into one of your boats and back to Rip Rap beach."

Once Robert and his boats were gone, John walked back to where David was studying the line of dead men. "Any idea what happened here—why somebody would lay them out like this?"

"No." David pointed toward the water. "There are a lot of foot prints between here and the sea where several ship's boats came ashore." He looked to John. "It had to be as you and Robert were saying—that *Le Tiburon* came ashore and killed the men who were torturing Ben." He looked down at the nine bodies. "Since we didn't lay these bodies out this way, I…"

"Do you know semaphore, David?"

"A little. Why?"

"Look at those five bodies in the center. Instead of their arms being down at their sides like the two on each end, their arms are stretched out in various positions, like the hands of so many clocks." John kicked at one of their feet. "These five are signaling the letters C-O-L-J-S."

"Do you think that's supposed to mean something?"

"I assume it must."

David brought his lantern close to one of the dead men's faces. With his free hand, he wiped the man's bloody throat with a finger. The blood was fresh and the body was still warm. "I don't believe these are the men we killed yesterday morning, John."

"Oh?"

"This man's been fresh killed! They must have got into a fight before we got here, and their mates laid out the dead ones this way before the survivors went back to the trees."

John touched another of the bodies. It was the same. "Captain Steele needs to know about this as quickly as possible."

CHAPTER SIX:
The Yellow Kerchief

The ship's doctor had been tending to Ben Gunn's burns and bruises for a half hour when the rescue party rounded the last outcropping and stepped onto the north end of Rip Rap Beach. Robert was waiting for them.

John called. "How's Ben faring?"

"He's some bruises and a few cuts in his mouth where they hit him."

"What about the burns?"

"McKenzie told me that he'll have some serious scars from the irons, but other than the pain for a few weeks, that seems the extent of his sufferings." He turned and matched strides with the younger men. "The poor soul was unconscious most of the trip back."

"Most of the trip?"

"He'd cry out now and then and then fall back senseless."

"Was he able to tell you anything?"

"No—just raving about Long John Silver."

"Long John Silver? What did he say?"

"Nothing I could put together." Robert pulled back the flap and ushered John and David into the medical tent. Doctor McKenzie was applying a dressing to Ben's leg.

"Captain Jones, Mister Noble." He finished the wrap, secured it in place, and picked up the jar of honey. "He's doing much better."

John stepped to Ben's side and put a gentle hand on the old man's shoulder. "Enough that he can talk with us for a few minutes?"

"I'd rather he rested for now, Captain. I'm afraid of the strain the affair has had on his heart."

"I can talk with you, Captain Jones." The old maroon raised himself onto an elbow. "These burns aren't nothin' anyway." He pointed at the three rows of iron burns from his ankle to his upper calf. "Look at that. Straight as tattoos from my ankles all the way to my knees."

"I'll give you ten minutes with him, Captain but please no longer." With that, Adam excused himself and walked from the tent.

"It's obvious they tortured you to tell them the location of the treasure, Ben."

"They was wastin' their time, Mister Ormerod, cause you never told me where you buried the treasure."

Robert pointed toward the north shore. "Do you know anything about all those nine dead pirates next to the fires?"

Ben shook his head. "Last thing I remember before wakin' up here is my legs bein' burned the last time. I never saw any dead pirates."

"Robert told me you kept talking about Long John Silver."

"I always dream 'bout Long John Silver—ever since I freed him from the *Hispaniola*—but I don't remember talking about him last night."

"Thank you, Ben." John gave the old man a pat on his shoulder. "We'll leave you to Doctor McKenzie's care for now."

"Aye, Cap'n Jones." The old man lay back on the cot with a groan. "I'll be up an' aroun' afore the *Silver Cloud*'s ready to sail."

The three returned to the officer's pavilion where the cook was standing by to prepare their breakfast. John got himself a cup of coffee and looked across at the *Silver Cloud*. Robert stepped next to him. "Ben's going to be alright."

"That's not what's bothering me, Robert."

"You still think there's a spy on the Cloud, don't you?" John didn't answer. "Do you think Van Mourik's in league with Smoot?"

"I don't believe he's a spy, Robert, but he is a chronic braggart when he's drinking. There's no telling how many people he told what we're doing here."

"Hmm." Robert looked across at the ship where Van Mourik was eating breakfast. "That's why he's conspicuously absent from most of our staff meetings, right?"

"Right. It's best for all concerned that we control what Van Mourik knows and doesn't know."

"But I heard you telling him our departure will be delayed for at least another week. Why would you confide something like that when you know he'll tell everybody?"

"For exactly that reason. Consider it, Robert. Our secrets are reaching the pirates. If Van Mourik is the cause—and I hope he's not—he becomes the perfect conduit for relaying false information."

"John?" David stepped to the two. "When do you want me to go out to meet with Captain Steele?"

"As soon as we finish breakfast." John gave Robert a quick glance. "I want to know if he killed those twelve pirates last night, and I'm certain he'll want to know about the digging parties we're sending out."

"Should I tell him when we expect to load the treasure and depart?"

John thought for a moment while he searched the sea to the south. The *Eagle* was tacking slowly from the east to the west. "Only if he asks, and then I want you to tell him that our carpenters found some internal damage to the *Silver Cloud* that could take four or five more days."

"Do you really think it will take us that much longer, Captain?"

John shook his head. "There's evidence that we have a traitor on the *Silver Cloud*. If that is true, then we must keep our rigging and our knots tight until we find him, as they say."

An hour later, John, Robert, and David stood next to one of the ship's boats on Rip Rap Beach. David held a piece of parchment and his yellow kerchief was folded and stuffed in his pocket. Robert set a bottle of rum and three Cuban cigars in the boat. As directed, one of the cannons fired a quarter charge to summon the *Eagle* to anchorage.

☠ ☠ ☠

"Henry!" Captain Smoot stepped from his stateroom and called. "Henry Morgan!"

"Aye, Captain!" The orange-haired youth slid down one of the main shrouds and made a light-footed landing on the deck next to his captain. "The signal. You heard it too?"

"Of course, I heard it." Smoot wiped his mouth and shaded his eyes against the morning sun. "Come about, Henry, and take us to the anchorage. The *Silver Cloud* is going to pay us a visit."

"Aye, aye, Captain!"

Joshua returned to his stateroom and sat down across from Captain Steele. "Seems we're to have a visitor in a little while, Alan."

"Yes, it seems so."

"I just want to make certain you still understood what it will cost you and your men if you betray me."

"I know my duty, Captain Smoot."

"Good." Joshua picked up a piece of toast and stepped to the port window. "We'll reach our anchorage in half a glass." He stepped back to his chair. "Plenty of time to finish breakfast and to get topside to meet our guest."

"What are you going to do if it's somebody who recognizes you?"

"Oh, I'll be hiding close by where I can hear everything you and he say."

"Captain Smoot!" Henry pushed through the door and pointed north. "You better come see this." Joshua and Alan followed Henry to the main deck. "Look there, just below where they set up their shore battery."

Smoot studied the activity at water's edge. "Why I'll be! They've gone and dug up the treasure in broad daylight!"

"Aye!" Henry pulled his cutlass and stepped to Captain Steele. "And now there's no reason to keep this man alive anymore, is there?" He stepped beside Steele and raised his blade.

"Belay that!" Smoot caught Henry's hand. "You can kill him but not before we hear what our visitor has to tell us."

"But—"

"Lower your weapon, boy, or by John Flint's black heart, I'll split you from throat to crotch and have your heart for dinner!"

After several tacks, the *Eagle* dropped anchor at the break in the reef, near where the *Silver Cloud* lay the previous morning.

Smoot was now dressed in a colonial seaman's garb like the rest of the crew. He leveled his spyglass at the approaching boat and studied the young man at the helm. "Morgan!"

"Aye, Cap'n?"

"Take a look at that young man at the tiller and tell me if you remember him."

"Aye." Henry took the spyglass and studied the approaching boat. "That's Charles Noble's boy. He was there when his father gave us that map to take to New York."

Joshua turned to Alan. "Looks like you'll be on your own. Think you can handle it, without putting yourself in jeopardy?"

Steele gave a confident nod. "I can do anything I set my mind to."

"Of course, you can, but just to make sure you keep your word, there'll be a dozen cocked pistols about the deck."

"Ahoy, *Eagle*!" David Noble called from a hundred yards. "Permission to come aboard?"

Captain Steele stepped to the rail. "Permission granted, *Silver Cloud*!"

Steele called out. "How go the repairs on the *Silver Cloud*?"

"Going well, sir!" The man in the boat's bow threw his line aboard the privateer and they were hauled alongside. As David started up the ladder, Henry dropped down the forward hatch and Smoot stepped behind the mainmast. "If nothing else goes wrong, we could refloat her in a week."

"That long?" Steele extending a hand of welcome, and pulled the young Jamaican aboard.

"Our carpenters just informed us that they found some major damage where that ball *Le Tiburon* put through her amidship. That's going to take them another five or six days to repair before we can sail."

David flashed a look at the crew. "Mister Forrestal told me all about you and your fine ship, and I'm sorry now that I didn't take the time to come aboard when you were still at his docks."

"I hope Mister Forrestal's report on me wasn't all bad."

"On the contrary, sir. He tells me Mister Jefferson hand-picked you and your entire crew for this mission." David looked about at the crew for the first time and was struck with how rough they appeared. "Oh, Robert Ormerod sends his compliments." He turned and took the bottle of rum and the cigars from one of his men. "Shall we go to your cabin and enjoy a cigar and a glass of rum?"

"Uh…"

"Is there a problem, sir?"

"We're a close crew, David, so whatever you have to tell me, I would like them to hear also."

"Very well." David set the bottle and the cigars on the deck at Alan's feet. "A lot has happened since we arrived yesterday." David pulled the parchment from his pocket and started through the list. "As you know, once we were anchored outside the southern reef, Robert took us to Dorsal Rock on the north shore to dig up the treasure. The moment he plunged his sword into the ground, we were attacked by several dozen men. At the same time, somebody snuck aboard the *Silver Cloud* and released her anchor chain so that she drifted onto the reef. Then *Le Tiburon* attacked and you helped our two shore guns to drive her off. Then, when the tide allowed, we moved the Cloud over to the beach where we hauled her down so we could repair her damage." When he was finished, he looked at Alan. "So, now the *Silver Cloud* is careened for repairs, the island is crawling with men who are out to kill us for the treasure, Ben Gunn is recovering from his torture, and *Le Tiburon* is hiding somewhere repairing herself for her next attack.'"

"I don't mean to interrupt you, David, but I have to ask a question about the treasure."

"Yes?"

"Do you already have it aboard the *Silver Cloud*?"

"No." David gave Alan a smile. "Robert was convinced that we were being watched, so he took us to a false location to prove or disprove his theory."

"So, you don't have the treasure yet?"

"No." David looked at his list. "Captain Jones has a couple of questions."

"Yes?"

"When we dropped our anchor and went ashore, why did you abandon the *Silver Cloud*?"

"We arrived at Christiansted several days before you arrived, so we went ashore to buy provisions. Then, we began a search for enemy ships by searching the coast of Saint Croix and circling Dead Man's Chest twice every day to determine that the coasts were clear."

"But you left the *Silver Cloud* at anchor—a time that she was vulnerable to attack."

"I decided that your treasure hunters needed our support but halfway there, *Le Tiburon* arrived and began their attack."

"Okay." David looked at his list. "When we rescued Ben Gunn, we found nine fresh-killed men lying in a row next to the fire they used to torture him. Did you kill those men and lay them out that way?"

"Your question both offends and insults me, David. If I had killed those men while rescuing Ben, do you believe that I would just leave him there to die?"

"I did not intend to offend you, Captain Steel. Captain Jones and Robert Ormerod told me to ask you."

"Anything else?"

"Since you now know that *Le Tiburon* is somewhere nearby, Captain Jones wants to know why you have not hunted them down and destroyed them."

"Because my instructions were to guard the *Silver Cloud* against attackers, not to abandon her to hunt down those attackers." He paused. "Anything else?"

"Captain Jones wants to know what happened to *Le Tiburon*."

"Last we saw of her she was on fire and headed around the eastern tip of the big island." He pointed east toward Cotton Garden Point. "Like the *Silver Cloud*, she's probably hauled down on a secluded beach somewhere for repairs."

"One other thing."

"Yes?"

"Since you were not involved with Ben Gunn last night, then there must be another ship out here someplace."

Steele raised his brow. "Another pirate ship?"

"No telling until we spot her. Captain Jones wants you to make a circuit of the island as soon as you can, and report back to him."

"We'll do it as soon as you go back." Steele looked to the trail of men carrying boxes and shovels below the cliff.

David gave a knowing laugh. "I see you've noticed our digging party."

Steele wanted to question David but knew it would work to Smoot's advantage.

"We started yesterday after we got back from the north shore. You had to have seen the two we sent out in the afternoon."

"What's in the boxes those men are carrying?"

"Nothing. They're empty."

"Empty? Then why—?"

"That's Captain Jones' idea to fool the pirates."

"Fool the pirates?" Steele gave another quick glance toward where Smoot was hiding.

"Aye, like Aesop's fable about the little sheep herder who cried wolf."

"Oh?"

"He's sending out three or four of those crews daily to bury and dig up empty boxes. One of them will be carrying back the real treasure, but not even I will know which one."

Smoot heard every word from his hiding place. He stifled a curse.

"I suppose Captain Jones will want us to keep *Le Tiburon* occupied when you dig up the real treasure?"

"Of course, provided he knew when that would be. And mind you, I would tell you if I knew. It all depends on how soon the *Silver Cloud* is repaired and ready to refloat." David looked to the island as he considered. "There might be a way you could know that.

"Oh?"

David pointed to the crest of the hill. "As you know, we've two cannons on that cliff yonder. Captain Jones won't leave without taking them with us."

"I don't see why not, seeing as how…"

"Keep your ears open and your eyes peeled. When you stop hearing the caulking irons and you see those two cannons moved down the hill, then you can be certain the treasure's already aboard the *Silver Cloud* and she's ready to refloat. That's when you want to begin watching for Joshua Smoot and *Le Tiburon*."

While David was explaining about the cannons, one of Smoot's crewmen had stepped behind him. The pirate's eyes were fixed on the brightly colored kerchief hanging from David's back pocket. With a quick but indelicate jerk, the yellow square of cloth was out of David's pocket and behind the pirate's back.

Noticing the tug at his trousers, David's hand went to the now-empty pocket. "Hey!" David spun on the man and held out his hand. "Give that back!"

"No!" The pirate spoke with a schoolboy's impudence and began tying the kerchief about his unkempt hair, pirate fashion.

David made a lunge at the bandana, but the pirate twisted away and hid behind two of his mates. David turned to Alan. "Captain Steele!"

"Give it back!" The pirate gave a quick glance toward the mainmast and back to Steele. "Now, or I'll have you flogged!"

The pirate's face contorted with frustration. "But it's so purdy!"

"Now!"

The pirate looked at the mainmast. This time, Smoot's pistol was leveled at the man's chest. He pulled the cloth from his head and held it out to David. "Here then, an' a curse on the thing!"

The argument on deck was more than Henry Morgan's curiosity could stand. As carefully as he could, the young pirate poked his head from the forward hatch for a quick look at their visitor. But a quick look was all it took, for in that split second before Henry could duck away, David's eyes caught sight of the red hair and green eyes of the Charles Town wood carver and painter.

A flash of heat raced up David's back. "Captain Steele...is anything wrong?"

"Wrong?" Steele looked about to see what his young visitor had seen. "I don't believe so. Why do you ask?"

"Captain Jones..." David pulled the yellow kerchief from his pocket and began wiping his face and neck. He fumbled for the best words to say. "If you're short of any supplies, uh, he wanted me to offer you whatever you might need. That is, if you're low on anything."

"You can tell my good friend that we have everything we need." He looked down at the bottle and the cigars. "That's unless he'd consent to sending across more rum and cigars."

"Rum and cigars?" David knew these two captains hated each other. By Steele talking this way, it confirmed his suspicions about the situation on board the *Eagle*. "I'm sure he'd do that for a good friend like you."

"Then rum and cigars it is!" Steele took a step toward David. "Was there anything else Captain Jones wanted to tell me?"

"No, that was all. He just wanted you to know about the fake digging parties and to ask about those dead pirates on the north coast."

"Then convey my respects to your fine young captain, Mister Noble, and tell him I look forward to our reunion at Charles Town."

"Thank you, sir. I will."

As quickly as he could go, David was over the rail and into his waiting boat. As the oars took their first bite at the sea, Steele found Smoot's hawkish nose in his face.

"So, his father's trading my cannons for the treasure, is he? This is better than I ever hoped for."

Henry trotted down the deck and stopped next to the two. "How so, Captain?"

"Don't you see it, Morgan? I was planning on sending Pritchard and *Le Tiburon* against the *Silver Cloud* if they escaped from the Chest but…" Smoot paused to consider the implications of the new revelation. "Fate has finally smiled on me! We will not have to risk sinking the *Silver Cloud* in deep water because the treasure is destined for the Noble warehouses in Kings Town!"

"When do we tell Privy?"

"Not just yet." Smoot turned to watch the retreating longboat. "Matter of fact, I don't believe it's in our best interest that Pritchard ever knows."

"What?"

"If things go sour and the *Silver Cloud* escapes before *Le Tiburon* returns, we'll simply beat her to Kings Town and wait."

Steele could not resist making a comment. "You think you have it all figured out, don't you?"

"Ah, Captain Steele!" Smoot gave the man a toothy grin. "I forgot all about you for a minute there, what with all this wonderful news about the treasure and my cannons." Smoot gave a squint. "What was all that chummy talk between you and David Noble?"

"What chummy talk?"

"That best friend bilge! It sounded to me like you and this Captain Jones were twin brothers or something."

"He and I nearly came to blows about putting in at Virginia last month so he could visit a woman friend of his. He repented and I forgave him. I just wanted him to know for sure we were reconciled—Bible like."

"If I find out you and Noble have been trading signals—"

"And what if we were? You plan on killing me now anyway, don't you?"

Smoot toyed with the thought. "No, not just yet." Turning, Smoot ordered the sails set for the trip about the island.

CHAPTER SEVEN:
Van Mourik's Quakers

*A*top the hill, five gunners watched with mild interest the arrival of their first officer's boat at the privateer *Eagle*. They had heard the jokes about the yellow kerchief and had contributed their share of sarcastic comments about the young Jamaican's paranoia.

One of the half-naked gunners' mates straddled the larboard cannon with the spyglass at his eye. "Well, what's your guess, McCoy?"

"My guess?" The gunner gave a snort. "Noble's gone to reprimand Captain Steele for allowing *Le Tiburon* to attack the Cloud, and to ask about Ben Gunn and that line of dead pirates on the north shore last night."

The young gunner handed the spyglass to his superior. "Steele's sure to ask about that digging party down below us too." He gave a laugh and threw a small stone down the slope at his shipmates. "I thought this was bad duty—manning these cannons—but digging holes an' carrying empty boxes all day is a far cry worse. I just hope the effort isn't wasted on the pirates that are still on this island watching us."

McCoy studied the *Eagle*. "Baker, I don't think we could break wind without the pirates knowing about it." The three others on watch burst into laughter, and one of them bared his backside toward the hill above them. "And if you keep that up, Cooper, you're gonna take a pirates lead ball in the butt."

Baker took the spyglass from McCoy and stretched himself prone on his cannon to watch the *Eagle*. For some time, David Noble simply stood amongst the others on deck and talked. But then, something changed.

"McCoy!" Baker thrust the spyglass back at the senior gunner. "Take a look at that!"

"Damn! Do you suppose he just forgot and pulled it out by mistake?"

"No." Baker pointed. "One of the crewmen pulled it from his pocket and Captain Steele made him give it back." He paused. "What is he doing now?"

"He's still got it out and he's looking straight at us." McCoy lowered the glass. "Let's check our guns just in case." A moment later, both the cannons were sighted at the *Eagle*'s mainmast.

"He's leaving!" Baker turned and gave the senior gunner a questioning look. "Mister Noble just got into his boat and they've pushed off."

"Could be a false alarm, but we have our orders."

"We could send Easton down the hill to find out."

"Good idea!" McCoy turned to the lad. "Easton! You heard Baker! On the double, lad!"

The barefoot and half-naked powder monkey took off down the path at a gallop. John and Robert were already waiting on the beach for David's returning boat.

Easton hit the hot sand and ran for the two officers. "Captain Jones! Captain Jones!"

"What is it, lad?"

"McCoy wanted me to tell you that Mister Noble pulled out his yellow kerchief. It might be nothing, sir but—"

"We saw it too, Easton." John focused his spyglass on the *Eagle*. By now, the sleek privateer had set sail and raised her anchor.

Robert studied the departing *Eagle* from under a shading hand. "Can you see anything amiss?"

John was still watching David's approaching boat. "Nothing on the *Eagle*, but David is waving his kerchief and he looks worried."

A few minutes later, David's boat pulled within earshot of the beach. He stood from the tiller and called. "John! Robert! Something is terribly wrong on the *Eagle*!"

"What did you see?"

"I talked with Captain Steele, but everybody else on board is a pirate!" David leaped into the knee-deep water before the boat skidded onto the sand.

"Calm down, David and tell us what happened."

"We've got to get Dutch and ask him about one of the men at Mister Forrestal's shipyard." David began walking toward their hauled-down ship.

"Stop!" John grabbed the younger man by the arm. "Why do you think they're pirates?"

"There was a red-headed carpenter with green eyes named Henry Morgan who was working on the *Silver Cloud*. He was supposed to be part of the crew, but he disappeared the day Robert arrived from New York." David pointed seaward. That man is now a crewman on the *Eagle*!"

"Wait!" It was Robert. "Last year, Long John Silver sent two men to my home in New York to ask me to mark map. They kidnapped my four-year-old daughter to force me to comply. One of them matches your description of Henry Morgan."

"Who was the other man?"

"He said his name was John Manley, but since he was Silver's agent, I'm certain that was an alias." He looked at John. "Joshua Smoot and Henry Morgan have taken the *Eagle*."

John looked around to their careened ship. "I need to talk to Jack Van Mourik?"

Robert pointed across to where the breakfast line was just trailing off. "He always the first in line John, and now he's taking a nap in the shade of the Cloud."

"Easton!"

"Aye, Captain Jones?"

"Go fetch Van Mourik! Tell him to report to my pavilion at once!"

"Aye, aye, Cap'n!" While the lad galloped off, John turned and began walking. "David, how much do you know about Jack Van Mourik?"

"Only that he was brought aboard with a dozen other Dutchmen in case the British stopped us. Why?"

"I have a very bad feeling about the man."

The three officers stood in the shade of their canvas pavilion and watched Dutch lumber across the sand toward them. The man had acquired the disgusting habit of tying a small towel to a rope about his waist to wipe the sweat from his belly. The towel smelled worse than he did.

Van Mourik bellowed from twenty yards away. "You vant me, Captain Jones?"

"Mister Noble just got back from the *Eagle*, and tells me he saw one of the carpenters you were working with at Charles Town."

"Who dat be?" Van Mourik waddled under the pavilion.

David gave the fat man a nod. "He was the one with the green eyes and orange hair."

"Ja! Henry Morgan! A right fine woodcarver an' painter, dat boy."

"David told me that Morgan left the same day I arrived from New York. Did he say where he was going?"

"He went off to Savannah, he did. Tolt me der sea vas callin' to him again an' he knew a ship's captain down der who vood sign him on, ja?" Van Mourik turned to the young Jamaican. "What? Didn't he tell nobody he was goin'?"

John interrupted. "Why would he tell David?"

"Why, Henry tolt me dat he and Mister Noble go way back." The Dutchman gave David a questioning look. "Dat's what you tolt me, right?"

"I didn't know him, Dutch." He turned to John. "It was over a year ago. My father does a lot of trading at his yards, and I might have seen Henry there a couple of times."

"Slow down." He turned back to Jack. "Why do you think David knew Morgan before Charles Town?"

"Well, sure he knew Morgan! Master Noble told Mister Forrestal and me a story about Morgan—how he called himself the King of Tortuga, and that the lad was famous for killing crabs with a mangrove root."

"Oh that!" David gave a dismissive laugh. "It's just a story I heard from a seaman in Kings Town. I only guessed it was Morgan because of his looks."

John gave David a questioning look. "Robert."

"Yes?"

"A word." The two stepped away several yards. "Do you suppose the braggart got drunk and told Morgan about the treasure?"

"That's got to be it." Robert gave Van Mourik a look. "The man's a braggart, and a belly full of rum always loosens a tongue."

"So!" John stepped out into the sun and yelled at the sky. "Our ship is hauled down on an island that's crawling with pirates, and now we find out that the only ship sent to protect us is manned by pirates!"

"There can't be many pirates left from yesterday's battle, John."

"What?"

"There were about thirty of them, and we killed eighteen. We found the nine that kidnapped Ben Gunn, so there can't be more than three or four watching us."

"So, you're telling me that it could be worse?"

David called. "There is something else, Captain."

Both John and Robert looked at David. "What?"

"Captain Steele asked about the digging parties."

"And I suppose you told him?"

"Yes but it was before I saw Morgan."

John walked out into the morning sun and mumbled something vile toward the *Eagle*.

Robert called after him. "It doesn't matter, John! David didn't know when we'd be digging up the real treasure, so neither does the *Eagle*."

David called. "There is one more thing, John."

"Damn!" He looked back to his first officer. "What is it, David?"

David pointed up at the cliff. "I told Captain Steele that when we leave, we'll take those two cannons with us."

"Oh, Lord! All they must do now is watch for the cannons to come down the hill, and then they'll attack us!"

David stepped to him. "We could fool them with quakers."

"We don't have any quakers!"

"I know, Captain, but some of the extra men—the ones not repairing the Cloud—could build a couple. They could be carried up the hill the same night we're ready to leave."

John shook his head in frustration. "Well, at this point, I'm willing to try most anything!"

"Shall I assign some of the men to the project?"

"Not just some of the men, David." John pointed. "This would be a perfect job for Captain Van Mourik and some of his fellow Dutchmen. It doesn't take much talent to carve a square beam round and paint it black to look like a cannon."

Everything had been done that could be, but an uneasiness still gnawed at John's insides. It was the type of gnawing that told a man that more trouble was waiting on the next tide. He sat for nearly ten minutes staring at the words he had just penned in the log, wondering how many more obstacles would be thrown in his path. Could Captain Steele be rescued, and was he even worth the effort? Who killed those pirates on the north shore when Ben Gunn was tortured? Was there another pirate ship out there somewhere? Could the *Silver Cloud* be floated and escape the island without detection? The odds of the mission being completed seemed to diminish with each passing hour.

John closed the journal, stood, and walked across the sand to his damaged ship. "Barragan!" He waited a moment. "Seamus Barragan!"

"Coming!" The Irishman scrambled across the deck and looked down over the rail. "I'm here, Cap'n Jones!"

"I need to know how soon the *Silver Cloud* can be refloated." The Irishman hesitated. "A lot depends on your answer, Seamus, so be absolutely certain before you make me that promise."

"Aye." The Irishman looked back to the other carpenters for a moment. "The planking is repaired and it will take a couple more hours to caulk the seams, daub them with sap, and repaint them."

"What's the soonest she can be pulled from Rip Rap Beach and back to sea?"

"Tonight, on the rising tide."

"Thank you."

"Uh, Cap'n?"

"Yes?"

"Easton came to me about the quakers, an' it got me to thinking."

"Go on."

"Well, if we float the ship tonight on the tide, there's no use replacing the cannons with quakers."

"Ah." John looked up at the hill and back to the Irishman. "Tell me what you're thinking."

"Two things, Cap'n." Seamus gave a grunt. "Word is that there are three or four pirates on the island. They need to be found and killed before you dig up the treasure."

"I agree. Tell me the second thing."

"Just to confuse them a bit more, I've got the three powder monkeys set to hammering on the caulking irons through the night until the *Silver Cloud* is free and moving into open water. With the waning moon, it will fool the *Eagle* into thinking the repairs are not finished."

"Good ideas, Barragan." John pointed. "Now fix my ship."

While John turned back toward his pavilion, one of the young gunner's mates was running toward the officer's pavilion. "Captain Jones!"

"Over here!" The Scotsman stepped from the ship's shadow. "What's the matter, lad?"

It was Easton. He ran over to the ship, stopped, and pointed to the north. "We spotted another privateer holding several leagues off the north coast, sir."

"Oh no." John climbed the ladder and pulled himself onto the ship's deck. "Barragan!" John pointed aft. "The binnacle! Fetch me my spyglass!"

"What's happened, Cap'n?"

"Easton spotted another ship."

"Another ship you say?" The Irishman slid across the tilted deck and returned with the device. John pushed the glass into a pocket and climbed the shrouds to the top gallant yard with Barragan just behind.

"Who is she, Cap'n?"

"I can't make out her name yet, but except for her red sails, she's a twin to the *Eagle*." John fell silent when the ship's stern finally came into view. "Have you ever heard of the *Remora*?"

"No, sir."

CHAPTER EIGHT:
Treasure at the Manchineel Tree

The treasure of Dead Man's Chest had begun to live more in the realm of legends and myths than in the world of reality. Each time the story was served up over a pint of ale, the teller would add another helping of gold and an extra spoonful of blood and treachery, until even the oldest of seamen began to choke on the bloated meal. It was only the ballad that maintained the accurate tale. And what a tale it was! There was hardly a man on the seven seas who had not sung its words while he hauled on the sheets, buntlines, and halyards. Every man jack of them wondered after the treasure, hoping to somehow win a share of it. As each year passed, the chances of it ever being dug up diminished. But today, Captain John Paul Jones led the digging party that would finally unearth the legend.

The repairs to the *Silver Cloud* had gone just as Seamus had predicted. The shrill ring of caulking mallets against the hawsing irons that rammed the oakum between the planks testified to everyone on Dead Man's Chest and to the two Virginia privateers that the *Silver Cloud* was nearly ready to float. The *Remora* had maintained a position about the island exactly opposite from the *Eagle*, a tactic that puzzled John and his officers.

After the midday meal, the captain raised his glass in a toast. "To the *Silver Cloud* and her successful launching."

The other officers raised their glasses. "Here, here!"

John laid an unsealed letter on the table before the others. "This was left in my logbook."

Robert reached for it. "What is it?"

"It's our rendezvous instructions. We're to meet the second *Silver Cloud* a league north of Tortuga in four days."

He paused and scanned a list of duties he had penned on the back of the rendezvous letter. "We'll be splitting the crew in thirds, with one group staying here at the beach to make preparations to float the ship. The other two groups will climb the hill to dig up the treasure."

"What about Ben?" Robert pointed up the hill. "He deserves to be there when we dig it up."

"Of course, he does." John turned about to the doctor. "Is he well enough to go up the hill with us?"

The doctor shook his head. "I'd be worried his heart couldn't take the climb. But if we can find a couple of the men to carry him on a litter, then I'll permit it."

John looked about at the others, spread his arms, and gave a broad smile. "Then let's be about it!"

Within half an hour, forty-five men stood in a great circle amongst the waist-high brush and cactus, looking at a twenty-five-foot high manchineel tree. When last seen by Robert and his fiancée, the tree was a mere sapling, three feet tall and no thicker than a man's wrist. Twenty years and the torment of hundreds of storms had taken their toll on the once-straight tree. Its trunk was now nearly two feet thick and resembled a twisted collection of slimy sea creatures, oozing their caustic sap downward into the earth to mingle with the treasure.

"Listen up!" John looked about at the forty men while their conversations died into silence. "You're about to unearth the largest treasure ever buried in one location. It is going to be difficult work, but I can assure you that it will be worth every drop of sweat and every ounce of blood it demands of you. The weapons this treasure will purchase may be the one thing that frees the colonies and your loved ones from the death grip of Mother England!" He turned to his right. "Robert?"

The Yorkman stepped forward and pointed at the tree. "That manchineel tree is the center of the treasure. We need to clear the brush away for five paces in all directions from its trunk. Once all the casks and barrels are exposed, you'll switch places with the men with pistols, and they will carry treasure down the hill."

"Alright!" John stepped to Robert's side and called out. "Let the work begin!"

A cheer rose from the seamen as they attacked the brush. Within ten minutes, the large tree stood naked in the center of a thirty-foot circle of bare red dirt.

"Sir?" It was the bosun. "Do you want we should cut down the tree?"

"Only if we have to. Somehow, I don't feel it would be fair to kill the old soldier, especially after guarding this treasure for all these years. I'm sure it'll have to lose a few of its roots, but let's go as easy on it as we can."

When Robert and his friends buried the treasure, they had laid earth a cubit deep atop it. Nothing had changed, except that the tree had sent out its tentacles in search of the scarce water. At the end of the predicted two hours, all the treasure lay exposed to the late afternoon sun. Here and there—where a workman had torn a canvas bag—fifty and seventy-pound gold ingots reflected the sunlight as brightly as the day they were the artisans had cast and fashioned the various pieces in the smelters near the Aztec mines.

"I had no idea there was so much, Robert." John surveyed the spectacle before them. "Fate is a fickle mistress. If I could entice her to ensure the success of this mission, I'd be willing to offer most anything she wanted."

"Careful, John. She may be fickle, but she has an insatiable appetite for human pain. You may not be able to bear the cost she would require of you."

As Robert spoke his words of warning, two of the seamen placed a large chest before him and the other officers.

Ben Gunn reached out to one of the seamen. "Help me stand, lad." With an oath, Ben stood and hobbled to the chest. He looked at Robert. "May I open it?"

Robert nodded and struck the lock away with the point of a shovel. He stepped back to give the old man room. "Be my guest, Ben."

Ben pulled the last rusted fragments of the lock loose from the hasp and raised the lid. There was a collective gasp from those who could see the contents.

"This is all surplus, Master Ormerod!" Ben reached deep within the jewels and wiggled his fingers, just as a child would run his hands through a tub of beans.

"What are you saying, Ben?" John picked up several brightly colored jewels. "What do you mean that these are surplus?

"He's right, John." Robert knelt and looked up at John. "This is more than the million and a half we'd counted on."

"Then…" John knelt and whispered. "This chest of jewels doesn't have to be traded for the cannons?"

"No." He ran his hand through the gems. "Everything in this chest can be divided among the crew."

The sun was now two hours above the western horizon, a perfect angle for its rays to set the jewels afire in an aurora of radiant splendor. Even Robert—who had buried the treasure twenty years before—gasped at the sight. There were diamonds the size of walnuts and rubies that would choke a cow. Sapphires, aquamarines, emeralds, and topaz lay about as single gems mixed with sundry gold coins. And then there were the gems set in broaches, in necklaces, in bracelets, in crucifixes, in medallions, in rings both large and small, and in cups and plates of silver and gold—every design and use the human mind could contrive. Several leather pouches of black and white pearls lay about the edges of the open chest, spilling their precious contents between the larger gems. At its center, nearly hidden by the free stones, was a circle of gold discs, each standing upright in the sea of glitter.

Ben reached into the gems and pulled the object loose. "It's the King's crown!" Ben lifted the large ring of gold high into the air and turned about so all the men could see it. He held it out to Robert. "It's just like the one on Spyglass!"

John looked up from the chest. "There was another crown like that on Flint's Island?"

"There was, Cap'n Jones!" Ben lowered it toward his head. "But that other one is the queen's crown—nowhere as big as this one."

The crown was oval, with the head band nearly a quarter-inch thick and o solid gold. Atop the two-inch band were alternating crosses and sun-shaped discs—eight in all. At the center of each disc was set a ruby or an emerald, and around each of these was a circle of smaller precious stones.

Ben tried to set the crown on his head, but it was so large that it dropped past his ears and rested on his shoulders.

"Ha!" Robert burst into laughter. "You're a royal sight, indeed!"

Ben blushed and returned the crown to the chest. As he did, he noticed a folded piece of paper among the jewels. The old man picked it up and unfolded it.

"What have you there?"

"It's—" The old man began to shake and dropped the note as if it was on fire. "Oh Lordy! It's a death curse!"

"A death curse?" John picked up the paper and read the cryptic words out loud. "Beware the fires of Hell! He who first touches this treasure shall die within a fortnight and burn forever in the Lake of Fire!"

Ben stumbled backwards and fell to the ground. "I'll never live to see America!"

"Calm down, old friend." Robert took the note from John. "You're not going to die."

"But it's a death curse, Master Ormerod!" Ben stayed on the ground and struggled backwards to the line of brush. "I touched the jewels first, so the curse is on me!"

"It's only words, Ben." Robert held up the note. "There's no power in words written on a scrap of paper, except for what you allow them to have."

"That's easy for you to say, sir, 'cause the curse isn't on you!"

"But I can remove them, as simple as this." Robert tore the paper in eight pieces and threw them into the wind.

Ben ducked away from the fluttering scraps that were carried upward into the sky. "They're still on me, Master Ormerod!" Ben's mouth was frozen in a gasp of terror while he watched his death sentence flutter away over the ridge to the north.

Robert pointed into the sky. "The curse is gone, Ben! I'm afraid I'll be stuck with you for at least another decade."

"Enough of this!" John turned to the diggers. "I want each of you to lay down his shovel, go find your partner and take his rifle. We've a treasure to move and we are running out of daylight!"

Shortly after sunset, a stream of treasure-laden seamen began to flow like leaf-cutter ants down the easy slope toward Rip Rap Beach. They kept close to one another in order to avoid the need for lanterns that would alert the pirates that the treasure was finally moving.

It became quickly apparent to all but a few of the men that the cannon attack on the *Silver Cloud* had worked to their advantage. With the great ship hauled down on the dry sand, it cut the loading time to a fraction of what it would have been had the ship remained at anchor outside the reef.

By eight o'clock, the entire treasure was secured in the ship's lazarette. With the rising tide, and thirty-six of the crew's strongest oarsmen put their backs to the task of pulling the *Silver Cloud* clear of the sand of Rip Rap Beach.

"Careful there!" It was Barragan. "Give the boats time to pull her hull far enough off the sand so she floats free when she's upright!"

Once the ship's hull was far enough into the deep water, John ordered the beach crew to let out on their blocks and tackle to allow the mast to rise.

Within an hour, the great ship was pulled far beyond the north reef and before the eastern sky had begun to pink, the boats had pulled the *Silver Cloud* four leagues to the west of Dead Man's Chest.

CHAPTER NINE:
Escape and Bad Water

"**O**n deck!" The cry came from high in the *Silver Cloud's* upper rigging. "There's still no sign of *Le Tiburon* or the *Eagle*!"

"What about that third ship—the Virginia schooner with the red sails?"

"She's not there either, Captain!"

David shaded his eyes and searched aft. "They either didn't notice that we were gone, or they're waiting for the winds so they can stop to pick up those last four men they had on the island."

"Aye." John turned and looked into the sails. "Look! The winds are picking up. He pointed to the four boats that were still pulling them forward. "Order in the boats, David."

With every inch of canvas she could hoist, the *Silver Cloud* gained speed with every passing minute. By midmorning, the wind had shifted to larboard, bringing the *Silver Cloud* to a comfortable eight knots.

John paced nervously about the quarterdeck but stopped when he noticed the doctor standing at the aft ladder, shading his eyes against the sun.

"What's the matter, Adam?"

The doctor stepped close and whispered. "May I speak with you alone for a moment, John?" Doctor McKenzie was by nature a soft-spoken man, having been born to an aristocratic southern family and trained at the School of Surgeons in Boston.

"There's nothing Robert or David can't hear, Adam. What's troubling you?"

"Something's wrong with those men from the boats—the ones who were pulling us away from the island this morning."

"Go on."

"Well, at first I thought it was just the heat and their fatigue, but they've not gotten any better. No matter how much water they drink or how much they rest, it's as if they all caught falling sickness at the same time."

Robert stepped to them. "How many of them are affected?"

"They're all affected. Every last man."

"Is anybody else sick?"

"A few—maybe half a dozen." He was ashamed that he could not be more certain what was happening. "It might be the remitting fever, Captain but then…"

"What do your books say?"

"That's what's so confusing, Mister Ormerod. It's a lot like the fever, but then there's too much belly pain."

David gave a tilt of his head. "Did they come aboard sick, or did it start after they got below to rest?"

"They seemed fine when they came aboard, sir, except for being tired and thirsty."

"Find out what you can, Adam, and report back to me."

"I will."

The surgeon turned to leave, but John called after him. "Make sure they are given all the water they need. If it's the remitting fever, they'll need a lot more than normal."

"The water!" Adam spun about. "It could be the water!"

"Damn!" John cursed loudly, bringing a chill to all within earshot. "David, go with the doctor and inspect the casks." He turned to the bosun. "Pipe the men to assembly!"

Within three minutes, all but the sick crewmen were assembled on the main deck. A rumble of muffled conversation ran through their ranks.

"Pipe down there!" The bosun gave his captain a glance to make sure he was ready. "Captain Jones has some words for you!"

"I assume you all know by now that a large portion of the crew is sick. We don't know what it is yet, but Doctor McKenzie suspects that somebody has poisoned our water."

Another murmur ran across the deck and up the mizzenmast to one of the top men. He called down. "I told 'em we have a traitor aboard, Captain Jones!"

John looked up and called back. "We don't know that for sure! Doctor Mckenzie will be reporting back to me as soon as he inspects the casks. Until we know for sure, I don't want you to drink any water."

"What about water taken from the main supply before we sailed, John?" It was Robert. "If someone poisoned the main casks this morning, the water up here on deck shouldn't be contaminated yet."

"You might be right." John turned back to the assembled crew. "Mister Ormerod has suggested that there may be some good water aboard. If any of you drew water prior to our sailing this morning, I want it turned over to Doctor McKenzie for testing."

Robert stepped to John's side. "I want to see those water casks too."

A few minutes later, John and Robert found David and Adam in the bilge. The younger of the doctor's two assistants sat atop one of the massive casks.

John called up to the young man. "Have you found anything?"

"We've a traitor all right!" The assistant held up a hand with white powder on his fingers. "And from the looks of it, he's done a thorough job."

"Come down and show me that!"

The young man jumped to the deck. "Look at this." He held out a moist handful of freshly cut wood shavings to his Captain. "Our saboteur has drilled a hole in the top of every cask and dumped in some sort of poison."

John turned to Adam. "How long before you know what it is?"

"Ten to fifteen minutes if it's common. Longer if it's something more complicated." Adam gave the powder a close look. "I won't know for sure until I run my tests, but I'd wager it's strychnine—rat poison."

"Damn him!" John turned and stared aft between the casks while he pondered their situation. "I've ordered all hands to turn over their personal water supplies to you. Is there a way to test it?"

"Once I know what he used, yes." Adam scraped together a small sample of the powder and placed it in a folded piece of paper. "With any luck, I'll have an antidote in my supplies."

By noon, fully half the crew had been stricken with stomach cramps and burning throats. Captain Jones ordered activity aboard the ship reduced to the bare minimum in order to reduce the need for water.

"Captain?" Adam stepped through John's open door. "It's strychnine."

"Is there an antidote?"

"My medical books call for emptying the stomach, and then drinking charcoal and permanganate of potassium—"

"I don't need to know all the details, Adam. Do you have what you need to make them well?" The doctor didn't answer. "Well?"

"The saboteur knew exactly what he was doing, John."

"Which means?"

"He knew it would take a lot of water to save these men's lives, and that would force us to make landfall to find a fresh water supply."

"Landfall." John looked at the chart spread on his table. "Now that we're away from Dead Man's Chest, their only hope of taking the treasure is to sink us in shallow water." He looked up at the doctor. "How much good water do we have?"

"Fifty, maybe sixty gallons at most. That's only going to last through tomorrow morning."

"I was afraid of that." John looked down at the chart. "Would you ask David and Robert to join us? We've several important decisions to make."

"As you please, sir." Adam turned to leave but hesitated. "Might I have a half-hour to check something first?"

"A half-hour?"

"I just remembered something I heard at school about rat poison. That should give me enough time to test my theory on a couple of the sick men."

At four bells in the early afternoon, Adam was followed into the master's cabin by David and Robert.

"Have a seat, gentlemen." John gave the doctor an enquiring look. "Well? Did your theory prove well?"

"Yes, it did. It's a crude poison, just as I suspected. My theory was that sugar-based alcohol might counteract its effects, or at least give some relief."

"And?"

"I was right. The three men I tested are improving as we speak."

"Then, you're telling me that we aren't going to lose any men?"

"Yes, but with a caveat."

"Oh?"

"If we do not get to a supply of fresh water before noon tomorrow, the affected men will begin to die." The doctor pulled a note from his pocket. "Oh, we've lost two pigs and a half dozen chickens."

"Hmm." John paused and then looked back at Adam. "Do you think the poison had time to get into the animals' flesh?"

"Probably not. Why do you ask?"

"Well, since the cook has to slaughter three or four pigs every day anyway, we haven't really lost anything."

"We can't eat them, Captain." It was David. He had an apologetic tone.

"Oh? And why not?"

"Because I had them thrown over the side."

"You what?" John jumped to his feet.

"They died of the rat poison, so I figured they weren't safe to eat, and we couldn't have them rotting on the ship.

"You fool!" John turned and looked aft into the ship's wake. "Don't you realize what you've done?"

"It's water we're short of John, not meat."

John spun on the younger man. "You've just told Joshua Smoot and those other two ships that their plan has worked!"

"What?"

"He's right, David." Robert pointed aft. "You've given the best possible signal to Smoot and the others that he's succeeded in poisoning our water. Now they know we'll be forced to find an island large enough to have a river."

"I'm sorry, John. Is there anything I can do about it?"

"No! It's too late to go back for them. It's more important that the crew gets fresh water than worrying whether the pirates know about our dilemma." John looked down at the chart.

Robert finally broke the silence. "John, you know my position on the cannons, so I may as well not mince words. The pirates are frustrated. They lost us once, and they will not be so careless the next time. You were correct earlier when you said that if they can force us to pull close to a river mouth, they will try to sink us in the shallows where they can retrieve the treasure at their leisure. I say we sail on to the rendezvous."

"But the men will die without water, Robert."

"It's a choice we have to make, Adam. The loss of a few men's lives is just part of the price the colonies must pay for the cannons and the freedom we're hoping they may bring."

"That's not a choice I will make, Robert! Without a new supply of water, most of those who drank the bad water will be dead in two days."

"But you told me that alcohol will counteract—"

"Not without several gallons of fresh water per man! We've no choice but to find a river!"

Before Robert could answer the doctor's objection, there was a knock at the door.

John welcomed the momentary diversion. "Come!"

The bosun stepped through the door and stood at attention. Several others remained in the passageway, one of them wearing shackles and chains.

"We caught the traitor, sir, and it's just like we figured."

"Who is he?"

"Jamison—the carpenter's mate who replaced that man who was killed a week before we left Charles Town."

"How did you find him, and why do you think he's the traitor?"

"One of the powder monkeys was cleaning up and noticed water leaking from one of the sea chests. When I pulled everything out, there was a false bottom where he had kept himself a supply of clean water." He held up a leather bag with white powder on the edges. "I also found this."

The doctor reached out. "I'll take that."

"Bring him inside."

The large bosun pulled the door open, grabbed the prisoner by his chains, and pushed him to the center of the cabin. "On your knees, traitor!"

John stepped in front of the man. "Is he correct? Are you working for Joshua Smoot?" The man would not answer. "There was a third ship at Dead Man's Chest—the same as the *Eagle* but with red sails. Who is that?"

"He isn't talking, Captain." The bosun gave the man a kick to the leg. "Not even when we beat him."

"Well, perhaps a few days in irons up in the hot sun will loosen his lips. Chain him to the mainmast and give him all the water he needs."

The doctor protested. "But Captain Jones—"

"We have six casks in the hold, Adam. Surely, we can afford a few gallons for our prisoner." Jamison gave a weak cry that sounded more animal than human. "Do you want to say something, Jamison?" John bent and put his ear near the man's mouth.

"I'm from Savannah. I've never seen that ship with the red sails."

"Then tell me about Captain Steele. What does Captain Smoot plan to do with him?"

"He couldn't know that, John. He hasn't had any contact with Smoot since before we left Charles Town."

"Robert's right." John looked to the bosun. "Take him up and nail his chain to the mainmast."

"And the water, sir?"

"Give him all he wants, as long as it's from the main casks." John bent down and whispered to the traitor. "I like how Moses put it, that when a criminal is caught, he will be made to pay a life for a life, an eye for an eye, a tooth for a tooth, a hand for a hand, a foot for a foot, a burning for a burning, a wound for a wound, and a stripe for a stripe." He paused. "If Moses were here, I believe he would add to that list, a poisoning for a poisoning." John stood and pointed. "Take him." Once he was gone, John turned to the doctor. "When Jamison finally begs for the poisoned water, give him one ration of our good water."

"But why, John?" It was Robert. "Jamison intended that we drink the bad water and die."

"It's because we're better than he is." John walked to his table and looked at the chart again. "I'd like to return to our former conversation, gentlemen. Are there any more suggestions?"

"First, tell us how far we can sail between now and noon tomorrow?"

John made a quick calculation, spread the calipers, and held them up to Robert. "If the winds hold for the rest of today, and pick up again in the morning, we can go this far."

"Where are we now, John?"

"Here." John put one of the points on the map, and as they watched, he set the other point down and scribed an arc. "That is Puerto Rico, and that is the Luquillo River. That's where we will take on a new water supply."

"We can't stop, John!"

"But you heard the doctor, Robert. Without a fresh supply, most of the men who drank the poison will die."

"If we stop at that river, *Le Tiburon* will attack us in the shallow water, and everything will be lost." Robert spun on the doctor. "And once we're sunk, the pirates will kill every one of us!"

"I don't understand, Robert." Adam looked around at the others. "What possible gain would there be in harming us after they have the treasure?"

"You really don't understand pirates, do you, Adam?"

"All I understand, Robert, is that the lives of this crew should be our immediate concern." He touched the map. " If we do not get that fresh water, and very quickly, a third of the crew will be dead or dying in two days. The rest will be so weak that they will not be able to fend off the lightest attack. Smoot's going to get the treasure either way. It's our choice whether we come through this alive or dead!"

"Horse feathers!" Robert pointed aft. "Those pirates know that as soon as we trade the treasure for the water we need, we'll turn and come after them to take it back."

John stepped back to the map and touched a line on the north side near the eastern tip. "The Luquillo River would still be very risky, but according to the chart, the water there is deep! We can make a series of slow passes to load and offload the boats, and still be able to maneuver if attacked."

Then..?" Adam looked at Robert. "Could you agree with that?"

"Like Captain Jones said, it will be risky, but I can see that it will provide the answer to both of our concerns."

"Good!" John turned to his first officer. "David, set a course for the northern tip of Puerto Rico."

"Aye, aye, Captain!"

John turned to Adam. "Tend to the sick, Adam. Since we'll be getting a new supply, use the rum and as much water as you need."

"Thank you, John." He turned to Robert. "Please forgive me for my harsh words. I know you care for both our crew and for the mission."

"Your apology is accepted." He looked about at the others. "Getting the treasure to the rendezvous point and then getting the cannons to our military is my primary concern. But I can also see that a healthy crew is essential to that end."

John waited a moment and turned to the doctor. "How's Ben?"

"Much better, sir. His fever has broken, and I've done everything I can for the burns on his legs."

"He didn't drink any of the poisoned water, did he?"

"Fortunately, no."

"Do your best for him, Adam." As the doctor and David left, John turned to Robert. "You and Ben are close, aren't you?"

"He's like a father to me in some ways, John, and like a son in others."

"Oh?"

"When this war finally starts, thousands of men will die painful and some-times obscure deaths. If I should lose Ben Gunn, the world will see his death as one of those obscure deaths. To me…" Robert's voice broke.

"Aye." John picked up his glass and pitcher of water. "I believe I'll pay Ben a visit."

By the time the course change was passed to the helm, John had reached Ben Gunn's cabin with the water. He tapped gently at the half-opened door. There was no answer, so he pushed it open with his shoulder and stepped inside.

"Ben?"

"Come in, Cap'n Jones." The elderly man's voice was just above a whisper.

John filled the tin cup with water and handed it to the old man. "We've had a meeting, and decided that with the poisoning of our water supply, our only option is to make for a river on the northeast coast of Puerto Rico."

"Which river were ya lookin' to use, sir?"

"The Luquillo River."

"And what about those three pirate ships that are following us?"

"We were able to sneak away from Dead Man's Chest during the night without them noticing."

"They won't give up, Cap'n. They'll keep coming and attack us when we anchor for water."

"We won't anchor."

"Then…" Ben gave John a questioning look.

"My plan is to keep the *Silver Cloud* moving, and slow only enough to rendezvous with our boats to offload the empty casks and load the full ones."

"Van Mourik told me about the poison, Cap'n." Ben drank the cup empty. "How many men have we lost?"

"None yet, and with God's help—" John was cut off by yelling from the deck. "I have to go!" Once on deck, John called to David. "What's happening?"

"It's the *Remora*—the privateer with the red sails! She is on a course to intercept, and she's closing fast!"

"And what of the *Eagle* and *Le Tiburon*?"

"No sight of them yet, John."

"Something has delayed them." John searched the deck for his gunner. "McCoy! Man the guns!"

CHAPTER TEN:
Long John Silver's Letter

There was no sense in running from the *Remora*. It was common knowledge that a Virginia privateer could easily outrun a square-masted brig. Within minutes she would easily close with the *Silver Cloud* and maneuver into a position to attack the larger ship from either the stem or the stern.

John studied the activity aboard the *Remora* for several minutes. He lowered the spyglass and turned to the other officers. "Gentlemen, we've a golden opportunity before us which we simply can't afford to pass up. I don't expect we'll ever find our three pursuers separated like this again, so I intend to engage and sink the *Remora*." John looked to David. "Pipe the crew to general quarters and clear the decks for action."

The deck came alive. Whereas half a dozen teams of men had been pulling at the sheets, there were now over sixty men running for the ladders that led to the gun deck and their battle stations. Many of the men who had been suffering the ill-effects of the strychnine poisoning took their places with the rest of the crew. John stood with his hands on the starboard rail.

"I can't figure her, Robert. She's on a course to intercept us, but her captain hasn't ordered her gun ports opened."

David stood several feet behind the two older men. "Maybe she's not who we…" He checked himself when the two turned to look at him.

John took a threatening step toward his young friend. "You talk as if you know something about the *Remora*." He looked back at the fast-approaching ship and then continued his interrogation. "Do you?"

"It's just that there's something strange about her." David looked to Robert and back to John. "You two sense it also, don't you?"

"We all do, but until we know better, she'll be treated exactly like the *Eagle* and *Le Tiburon*." John looked forward to where McCoy was standing by. "You've an order to give, David."

The first officer looked to the *Remora*, and then forward to where McCoy waited. "McCoy! As soon as the *Remora* is in range, I want one warning round put across her bow!"

"Say the word and I'll take off a foot or two of her bow sprit, Mister Noble?" The gunner gave a laugh and was joined by the rest of the gun crews.

"No!" David gave his captain a nervous look. "We don't want to provoke them into firing on us, do we?"

"But I want them provoked, David."

David turned and shouted the order forward. "Make it close, McCoy, but don't hit them!"

The gunner gave a quick salute and dropped from sight. He was met by another muffled cheer from the bowels of the ship. Ten seconds later, there was the roar of a six-inch cannon. Then, as all hands watched with certain expectation, a column of water leaped into the sky from under the *Remora*'s bowsprit, showering her foredeck with brine.

"Well done, David!" John raised his spyglass at the *Remora*. "Now we'll see what she intends to do!"

"They won't fight us, John." David pointed. "Look!"

A white flag climbed the signal and the captain of the *Remora* called out. "Ahoy there, *Silver Cloud*!" The voice was strong and deep, with an unmistakable Scottish brogue like the one that John had been working so diligently for the past year to lose. "Daniel Archer here! Have I permission to come across?"

John gave David another questioning look. He turned, raised his speaking trumpet, and called back. "Aye, but be warned that we've another twenty cannons trained on your vessel!"

"Thank you, sir! Let me assure you that you will not be needing any armament against us!"

While the two called back and forth, a six-man boat was already lifting from the deck of the *Remora* to transport Captain Archer across. "I've a gift for you, Captain Jones—a gift that'd tempt a Papist out of his hassock."

"You know my name! Have we met?"

"No, we haven't, sir, but we do have a mutual acquaintance!"

"I'm anxious to learn who this person is, Captain Archer!" John moved closer to David's side as he continued to exchange shouts with the *Remora*. "Make haste, Captain Archer, for we have two pirate ships that will be closing with us shortly if we tarry!"

John turned to David. "You have some explaining to do." David remained silent, so John continued. "You've known about the *Remora* all along, haven't you?"

"Since my father has the cannons, he knows everything about our mission and where we are to rendezvous with the cannon ship. I told him about Mister Jefferson sending the *Eagle,* so he must have figured to protect his interests by sending his own ship along."

"Damn you, David!"

"Why are you cursing David, John?" Robert stepped across to the two. "What's the lad's done now?"

"His father owns the *Remora.* Charles Noble sent her to be our protector." He pointed at David. "My first officer knew it and waited until now to tell us."

"Who else is in on this?"

David looked down at John's half-drawn sword. "John, do you remember the day we met at Silver Jack's Tavern?"

"Yes."

"Do you remember the old innkeeper who befriended us?"

"The white-haired man with the articulated wooden leg?"

"Wait!" Robert gave David a push. "An old man with a wooden leg and a tavern called Silver Jack's?"

"I remember." John turned to Robert. "His name is Jack Bridger, and he's David's uncle."

Robert pulled his knife from the scabbard and held it at David's face. "Is it his left leg?"

"It's time to stop playing games." John drew his sword and put the tip to David's chest. "What is your uncle's real name?"

Before David could answer, there came a lusty greeting from forward. "Greetings gentlemen!" Captain Archer climbed onto the main deck of the *Silver Cloud* with a velvet bag the size of a woman's purse. "And greetings from my employer and your protector, Long John Silver!"

David backed away from John's sword. "The *Remora's* arrival was as much a surprise to me as it was to you, John."

"The lad's telling you the gospel, Captain Jones!" Archer strode aft, holding out a sealed letter. "Neither John Silver nor Davy's father told him I was coming to dead Man's Chest."

John took the letter, broke the seal, and read aloud.

Dear Captain Jones:

First, allow me to congratulate you for accomplishing what hundreds have tried at and failed. You are about to hand over to me the legendary Treasure of Dead Man's Chest.

That may stick in your craw, good sir, but we are all winners in this exploit. The Colonies will have their cannons, you and David will get your naval commissions, and Charles and I shall have our long-awaited rewards. Please do not feel badly that you have been manipulated and oft deceived. There was no other way to accomplish what you and your comrades have done.

Until we meet again—and that shall be sooner than you think—I am your true friend, humble servant, and greatest admirer.

Long John Silver

Robert reached for the letter. "Let me read that!"

John handed him the letter and returned his sword to its sheath. "So that sweet old innkeeper, Jack Bridger, is the infamous pirate, Long John Silver?"

Archer nodded. "You didn't know?"

John shook his head. "I expected someone much more…" John searched for the words.

"A bloodthirsty cutthroat?" Archer finished John's thought and gave a hearty laugh.

"Well, at least somebody who *looked* like a pirate!"

Archer held out the velvet bag to John.

"What's this?"

"It's Captain Silver's special way of saying thank you, Captain Jones. He told me he promised it to you when you were in Kings Town."

John untied the knot and pulled a bottle of Scotch whiskey from the pouch.

"It took him until now to locate just the right bottle—one from the distillery near your birthplace in Scotland."

"Yes, it is." John turned the bottle around and read the label. He looked up at Archer. "I assume I will be able to thank Mister Silver personally in a few days."

Robert turned to Captain Archer. "What can we expect from John Silver when we reach the rendezvous? Are we to be killed?"

"For the treasure? Why no, sir!" Archer had hoped the bottle of spirits and his good humor would relax his hosts. "Silver may be a pirate, but when he gives his word on a thing, he'll never go back on it. You'll get your cannons, as long as he gets his treasure."

"No tricks then?"

"None, sir!" Archer gave a slow shake of his head. "There'd be no point to it."

There was a moment of uneasy quiet as the two captains studied each other. Finally, Archer spoke. "I'd think my saving that old man on the north coast of the Chest would have convinced you of my good intentions, Captain Jones."

"So that was the *Remora*?"

"Aye, that was us."

"It would have helped if you had left us a message on one of the bodies."

"I did!"

"Oh?"

"Didn't you see the semaphore?" Archer was sure someone in the *Silver Cloud*'s crew would have picked it up.

"The dead pirate's arms?"

"Aye!"

John looked to David. "What were they?"

"There were five of them, Captain. I believe they spelled out O-C-J-L-S."

"No!" Archer turned to John. "They were C-O-L-J-S." Nobody ventured a guess, so Archer continued. "They stood for 'Compliments of...'" He paused when he saw Robert's expression change.

"Compliments of Long John Silver!"

"Ah! I knew there was a clever one amongst you!"

John pointed back toward Dead Man's Chest. "If you wanted us to know you were responsible, then why didn't you just spell out your ship's name? There were more than enough bodies!"

"And tell Smoot's men too?"

John considered for a moment. "No, I suppose you did all you could."

"And that's the only way John Silver would have it."

"There was a quiet laugh." Robert looked aft to where Archer had left his boat. "I have the sense that the old pirate is among us."

"I am, Robert!" John Silver stood on the ladder just high enough to see onto the deck. "If you promise not to shoot me or run me through, I'll come aboard and we can discuss our business like the gentlemen we are."

"My God!" Robert pushed past David, pulled his pistol, and fired it at the old man. It missed to the left. He threw down the pistol and continued forward with his knife drawn.

John called to the nearby seamen. "Restrain Mister Ormerod!" Before he could reach his intended victim, the two seamen grabbed him by the arms and pushed him back to the opposite rail.

"I'm nobody's god, Robert." Silver chuckled while he pulled his bulk up and onto the deck. "But I'm certainly your benefactor."

"If these men weren't holding me back, I'd choke you to death with my bare hands!"

"Well then, you make me thankful for their restraining hands!"

Captain Archer stepped to John Silver's side. "Gentlemen, may I introduce the unofficial Mayor of King's Town, and my employer, Long John Silver?"

Robert gave a jerk at the man on his right arm. "Your mayor is a murderer! He's the one who sent Joshua Smoot and Henry Morgan to New York! They kidnapped my daughter and held her for ransom to force me to mark and sign his map!"

Silver gave his articulated leg a slap and then walked about in a circle. "Aren't I a vision o' heaven Robert, in my new waistcoat and fancy articulated leg?"

"More like a vision from hell, you thieving cutthroat!"

"'Thieving cutthroat'?" Silver echoed with feigned disappointment. "You wound me, Robert."

"But that's exactly what you are! A murdering thief and a cutthroat!"

"And I suppose you and my little brother are respectable merchants?"

"Of course, we are!"

"Wrong!" Silver leaned close to the Yorkman. "We're all cut from the same cloth—you, Charlie, and me. The only difference is that your lines follow a slightly different pattern."

"Never!"

"We both deal in valuable goods and we both ask the highest price the market will bear. As I see it, the only place we truly differ is that I take a slightly higher percentage of the swag than you."

"But there is a difference!" Robert struggled again to get loose. "You and your kind kill for the goods you take!"

"And what if I were to purchase a letter of marque like those colonial pirates you deal with?"

"Nothing would make you—"

"Or what if I were a Spaniard? Would you still hate me as much?"

"A Spaniard?"

"Aye, a Spaniard! Ten years ago, when we were at war with them, I heard you blew up at the mere mention of the race!" Silver took a long breath and waited for Robert's answer. "At a loss for words, Robert?"

"Calm down, you two!" John stepped between them. "We've more important things to accomplish than settling old scores."

"It cuts my soul in half to know you're finally going to get the treasure."

"And did you ever doubt I would, Robert?"

"Yes! I figured you would be shoveling coal in hell by now, provided the Devil would allow you into the place!"

The thought of tangling with Satan, one-on-one, amused the old pirate. His lips curled back in a wry smile, revealing the row of large white teeth. "But I believe Satan's got his hands full dealing with John Flint."

"Enough!" John turned to Silver. "I need to know several things from you, Mister Silver."

"Such as?"

"Why are you on the *Remora* rather than the *Silver Cloud* that is carrying the cannons. And what are we going to do about *Le Tiburon* and the *Eagle*?"

"I'm on the *Remora* because of the treasure."

"But that wasn't your mission! You were supposed to meet us at the rendezvous."

"I have men whom I trust to do what I've told them to do, Captain Jones, unlike your Mister Jefferson."

Robert was still restrained. "What do you know about Jefferson?"

"Nothing directly, but from what I've seen, he isn't a very good judge of character."

"What do you mean by that?"

"Didn't he choose the captain of the *Eagle*?"

"Go on."

"Well, I'd say it was a poor assignment by the way Captain Steele allowed *Le Tiburon* to get close enough to disable the *Silver Cloud* like that?"

"Smoot's not on *Le Tiburon*, Uncle Silver."

"Oh?"

"He and Henry Morgan are on the *Eagle*, or at least they were when we departed the Chest."

Silver looked at his nephew. "A lad with green eyes and flame-red hair?" David nodded. "Well, I'll be a maroon's armpit!"

Robert twisted loose from one of the men but was grabbed by another. "I told you that he sent them to me!"

"And I put a dead little girl in the sail loft, set it ablaze, and took your daughter to feed the ducks. And then I delivered her to you and Moira with my letter that explained everything."

John turned to the bosun. "Take Mister Ormerod to his cabin and place two guards at his door. Keep him there until Captain Silver is gone."

"Aye, Cap'n."

John pointed aft at the companionway. "Take him." A moment later, Robert was gone.

Silver gave a huff. "Thank you, Captain Jones. Now where was I?"

"Smoot and Morgan."

"Ah, yes! I met Morgan briefly on Tortuga, and a few years later, the two came to Kings Town on a quest."

"What kind of quest?"

"Smoot wanted to know where his father—John Flint—was buried. Our deal was an exchange—Flint's gravesite for the map to the treasure." Silver looked east. "So, Joshua Smoot's aboard the *Eagle* and playing your protector?"

"Aye."

"You know of course, that he'll sacrifice *Le Tiburon* and most of his men if he has to in order to take your ship?"

"That's why I want to get under way as quickly as possible. Would you and Captain Archer, please return to your ship?"

Silver stroked his beard in thought. "Smoot doesn't know about the second *Silver Cloud*, does he?"

"Yes, he does." John looked at David.

"After the *Silver Cloud* was damaged, I rowed out to tell Captain Steele what was happening, and what we expected of him." He looked at John and back to Silver. "Before I realized they were pirates, I told him everything, even the rendezvous."

"Ah!" John Silver pinched his lower lip between thumb and finger. "That means he might wait until we unload the treasure at King's Town."

David shook his head. "I believe he'll order *Le Tiburon* to attack us before then."

"I think David's right but not in deep water."

Silver held up a cautioning hand. "He could order *Le Tiburon* to attempt a boarding, after he's raked your rigging with shot. He only needs to disable the *Silver Cloud*, not sink her."

John pointed at the *Remora*. "It would be best for us if you would leave my ship, Captain Silver."

"Before I go, any special instructions for when the *Eagle* and *Le Tiburon* catch up with you?"

"We had a saboteur put rat poison in our water, so we will be stopping on the north coast of Puerto Rico to take on a new supply. You can play our protector if we're attacked."

"That's why I am here, Captain Jones."

As John Silver turned about to descend the ship's ladder, he noticed the crewmen who had been gathering on the main deck to get a look at the famous pirate.

Archer noticed that some of them were sick. "Some of your men look unwell, Captain Jones. Could you use a few of my men until your crew's stronger?"

"Yes, I could. I'd take a dozen topmen, if you could spare them."

"I'll order the exchange. If you'd like, I can take your weakest men aboard the *Remora* until we reach a place of refuge."

Within a half-hour the *Silver Cloud* had taken on the *Remora*'s crewmen and the two ships were underway. At John's request, David and Robert were waiting in his cabin.

"Well, well!" John closed the door and walked to the table. "As John Silver wrote in his letter, I've certainly been manipulated."

David shook his head. "We've all been manipulated, John, from the very beginning."

"From when you went back to Kings Town to deliver the five letters, you mean?"

"Oh no. He manipulated you and me from the day you arrived at the dock in Kings Town and walked into Silver Jack's Tavern."

"Silver Jack's?" Robert closed his eyes and exhaled in frustration. "My God, John. The name of the place should have warned you!"

"You forget that I'd never heard of Long John Silver before I met you and Ben. I suspected something when David told me about Silver on our way to Fredericksburg, but…well, I guess I chose to ignore it."

"He had to ignore it, Robert, just as I had to deceive him." David turned back to his captain. "John, be honest with us. Would you have thrown in with me if you knew a pirate was using us like this?"

John shook his head.

David turned to Robert. "And would you have agreed to lead John and me to the treasure if you knew my uncle was involved?"

"Never!"

"Answer me one more thing. Do the colonies need those cannons?"

Both men nodded.

"Now that you know it was Long John Silver all along, does it really change anything?"

John shook his head. "Not really."

CHAPTER ELEVEN:

Le Tiburon's Demise

A hand slapped Henry Morgan's face. "What the hell?" Henry jumped away from the mast, rubbed his face with both hands, and stared at his captain. "What was that for, Cap'n?"

"For that!" Joshua pointed to Rip Rap Beach. "Something's missing, Morgan!"

The lad looked around and rubbed his eyes. " They're gone! The *Silver Cloud*'s up an' gone!"

"That's right, Henry, and she got away while you were on watch!"

"But look, Cap'n!" He pointed to the cliff. "You told me that they would not leave the cannons on that cliff, and that as long as we heard them caulking her seams, we didn't have to worry about her leaving." He turned back to his captain. "They fooled us."

Smoot turned west and strained his eyes to locate his fleeing prize. The sails of the *Silver Cloud* were just now disappearing over the horizon. Smoot spun on Henry. "Maybe I should have let you skipper *Le Tiburon* after all." Smoot looked about toward the east end of Saint Croix. "Which reminds me—where is Pritchard? If the Cloud can be repaired in three days, then so can *Le Tiburon*."

"But they took a hit to their mizzen, Cap'n, not countin' the shot holes to her hull an' the fire." Henry kept his distance from his irate captain. "And then there's her men still on the Chest. They'll want to pick up their men from off the Chest 'afore they could begin to take up the chase anyway, so there's that besides."

"Those men can die there for all I care." Smoot looked up into the rigging. All the telltales and flags were hanging limp. "When the wind picks up, we're sailing to Cotton Garden Point to find *Le Tiburon* and have a parley with Nate Pritchard."

An hour later, the breeze morning breeze finally came across the sea to the privateer. While the crew raised the anchor and trimmed the sails trimmed for the reach toward the eastern tip of Saint Croix, Captain Smoot called out to his first mate. "Henry!"

"Aye, Captain!"

"Go aloft and with your spyglass and look for *Le Tiburon*!"

Rounding Cotton Garden Point, Henry called down and pointed. "On deck! *Le Tiburon* a league south at the next bay!"

"Can you tell their condition, Henry?" Joshua stepped to the rail and shaded his eyes. "Are they careened or afloat?"

"She's afloat, Captain, but all her boats are clustered about her waterline, so I'd say she's not ready to get underway yet!"

Twenty minutes later, the *Eagle* dropped anchor a hundred yards north of *Le Tiburon*. As Nate Pritchard and several of his crew pulled across to them, Joshua called out. "What is taking you so long?"

"There was a fire on the gun deck." He turned and pointed back at his ship "Our mizzen was nearly cut in half, so that had to be splined and wrapped or else it would break at the first heavy wind." Pritchard started to climb up the side of the *Eagle*. "What say we talk over a glass of rum?"

"No!" Smoot put a foot in the man's face. "The *Silver Cloud* left during the night with the treasure and is several leagues west by now."

"But we could hear the caulking irons through the night. How—"

"They fooled us, and now they're several hours ahead of us."

"Then we won't be able to catch them, even if we set sail right now."

"Oh yes you will."

"How?"

"The man who released their anchor and put them on the reef is still aboard, and I ordered him to poison their water supply the moment they got underway. They will be forced to stop at a river somewhere on the north coast of Puerto Rico. That's where you will catch them."

"Okay?" Pritchard stepped back down into the boat. "What do you want me to do when I catch them?"

"Now listen to me carefully Nate. We want the treasure. That means that the *Silver Cloud* cannot be sunk in deep water."

"I understand that."

"You were up close to them, so you could see that they have no cannons except those two they left on the island."

"Then…"

"You will sail ahead of us and disable them by taking out their rigging and their rudder." Once they are floundering, we will join you and together force them to surrender the treasure."

"You're certain they left their only cannons on Dead Man's Chest?"

"We just came from there, and the cannons are still where they were when they fired on *Le Tiburon*." Joshua pointed northwest. "You saw the *Silver Cloud* up close. Except for those two cannons they left behind, they have no guns."

"Ah!" Pritchard licked his lips. "Then, it will be like shooting fish in a barrel."

"Yes, so get back to *Le Tiburon* and chase them down."

"Aye, aye, Captain Smoot." In a moment, he was gone.

"Cap'n?"

"What, Henry?"

"The *Silver Cloud* has thirty-six hidden guns. Why would you tell Privy that they're unarmed?"

"Because that's what I want him to believe."

"But when he makes his attack…" Henry paused. "That's right. The *Silver Cloud* will take the treasure to Kings Town."

☠ ☠ ☠

With the setting sun, the winds decreased and stopped completely. Captain Jones stood atop the main royal yard and searched the eastern sea for the two pirate ships. Ten minutes later, he jumped down from the shrouds and walked to the helm where the other officers waited.

"There's still no sight of them, so I've decided that we'll anchor at the mouth of the river and spent the night replacing our water supply."

"Do you think this is the safe thing to do, John?" Robert looked north to the *Remora*. "Can we get underway and into deep water before *Le Tiburon* is upon us?"

"The pirates are subject to the same winds as we are, Robert." He wet a finger and held it up. "Dead calm, so if we can't move, neither can they."

"It's the right decision, Robert." Adam spread his arms. "This—anchoring here while we redeem our water supply—answers both of our concerns."

"Robert." John stepped to the Yorkman. "I promise that when our sails catch that first morning breeze, we will raise the anchor and be underway."

"Even if the water supply isn't full?"

"Yes."

"Thank you, John."

The *Silver Cloud* carried six boats of varying sizes—the smaller ones nested inside the larger ones to best utilize deck space. All six boats were put into service—coming and going with the casks with military regularity. While a chain gang rolled the various water casks about the deck of the great ship, the hoists were constantly raising the filled casks and lowering the empty casks to the waiting boats. Two hours before sunrise, the last casks were filled, rolled to the hatches, and lowered to the gun deck.

At Captain Jones' command, twenty sweeps were pushed out through their ports. While the anchor was raised from the sea, the *Silver Cloud* was rowed north into deep water where it would wait for that first morning breeze.

There was still no sign of either the *Eagle* or *Le Tiburon*, but everybody aboard the treasure ship knew they would be coming soon. As the sun rose above the eastern horizon, a light breeze filled the waiting sails, bringing to every ear the sounds of complaining ropes and leather against masts and yards—what sailors called the symphony of the sea. There was still no sign of their two pursuers—*Le Tiburon* and the *Eagle*. The *Remora*, by request of Captain Jones, had stationed herself a league to windward—the best position for a quick rendezvous should her assistance be necessary.

David turned about and studied the sea behind them. "How long do you figure before they'll catch us?"

"I'm surprised we haven't spotted them already." John looked about at the rising sun. "I'll wager ten crowns that the top watch reports two sails astern before noon."

The morning was uneventful aboard the disguised frigate, except that a rumor had escaped from the quarterdeck and run through the ship like a fox with its tail afire. Scuttlebutt was what they called it, and this rumor predicted a deep-water battle with *Le Tiburon* before sunset.

The young Scotsman sat down at his table to consult his charts and bring his logbook up to date. It might be his last chance to record the happenings of the last several days.

At just before ten o'clock there came an impatient hammering at John's door, along with the excited calls of one of the young gunner's mates. It was clear that his prediction had come true.

John pulled the door open. "How far astern are they?"

"It's *Le Tiburon*, Captain!" He pointed astern. "Two leagues, sir, and Mister Noble says with their greater speed, they'll be on us before noon!"

"Tell Mister Noble I'll join him presently."

"Aye, aye, Captain!"

By the time John had gained his position on the quarterdeck, the other four officers were assembled and awaiting his orders.

David asked the question they all wanted to ask. "Shall I sound general quarters?"

"Not yet, Mister Noble. I'm still convinced they'll not attack us in deep water."

"Uh…" Robert stepped close and spoke softly so as not to be heard by the crew. "As much as I hate to agree with John Silver, I feel he and David are correct."

"I can't run a ship on feelings, Robert."

"You forget, John, that I lived and served with some of those beasts. I know how the pirates think."

"And how do they think, Robert?"

"They're angry and frustrated. They've failed in several separate attempts to take the treasure from us, and they think our next stop is Kings Town."

"But a deep-water attack?"

"They don't have to sink us to take this ship, John." Robert pointed aloft. "They will fire on our masts and our rudder to disable us. Once we flounder, they'll pull us to their gunwale with grappling hooks and board us."

"Well, I'm still certain you're wrong." John looked to each of the other officers.

Ben Gunn called from the taffrail. "Cap'n Jones!"

"What is it, Ben?"

"I think you'll change yer mind when you see this."

"See what?" John took his spyglass from Robert and joined Ben aft.

Ben pointed. "Take a look at her flag, sir. It's red."

"Damn!" John lowered the glass and turned back to the others. "They've hoisted their no quarter flag. Seems that our Yorkman has predicted correctly once again."

The crew of the *Silver Cloud* had been in a state of readiness since they had departed Dead Man's Chest, so it took them only moments to begin transforming the hybrid ship into the man-of-war she truly was. The barrels of sand by each of the great masts were spilled onto the main and gun decks in preparation for the blood that might shortly flow over the planking. Doctor McKenzie and his two surgeon's mates descended to the interior of the ship where they began to lay out their medical tools and set two dozen cauterizing irons in a small stove. The bilge pumps were primed, and a continual procession of seamen brought an assortment of balls, grape shot, bar stock, and neatly tied flannel bags of black powder from the ship's bowels to the gun deck. Within an hour the *Silver Cloud* had completed its transformation.

"The guns are loaded and manned, Captain Jones!" McCoy gave a sharp salute. "Will you be wanting to make your inspection now, sir?"

"Aye." John gestured for the man to proceed him. The aft hatch had been removed, and a group of crewmen were crowded in the narrow passageway. John gave McCoy a questioning look.

"That'll be the two cannons I ordered set up in your cabin, sir. I apologize for disturbing your furnishings, but we'll need them if *Le Tiburon* positions herself to attack our rudder."

"No apology necessary, McCoy." John pointed forward. "Let's take a look at the rest of the guns." As the two entered the gun deck, the gun crews stood amidship between the starboard and larboard rows of cannons—all the cannons loaded and primed. The rammers, sponges, and worming irons were laid in neat rows between the guns, with small arms enough for every man stacked neatly against the masts. A cask of seawater stood next to each cannon in case of fire, and the racks of cannon shot looked like so many strings of expensive black pearls.

"You've done a good job, McCoy. If Mister Noble's done as well above deck, I'd say we're ready for anything they can throw at us."

"Aye, Captain. Those pirates don't have a chance against these fine lads o' mine—not a chance."

John turned about toward the forward ladder but hesitated. "While I'm down here, McCoy, would you show me where the doctor has set up his treatment station?"

"Aye, sir." The gunner turned aft. "According to one of my mates, he's on the deck below us, just aft of the mizzenmast step."

"In the tiller room?" John spun about and marched off toward the companionway, with McCoy at his heels.

"Did you not want him there, Captain?"

"Not unless it's the only place left on the ship!" At the base of the ladder, he swung about the great mast and stepped through a small hatchway. Several pairs of taut rope lines stretched down through the overhead and about pulleys to the great tiller. The doctor was giving his men a drill on cauterizing and amputations.

"Captain Jones!" Doctor McKenzie stepped away from the surgeon's mates. "You startled me. We didn't expect you to pay us a visit this early."

"Why have you set up here, Adam?"

"It looked like a good spot, sir. I figured we'd be out of the way, yet close enough to the gun deck and one of the ladders for quick access."

John turned to the gunner. "McCoy, is there an open space forward where we could move the Doctor and his men—maybe the forecastle?"

"Aye, sir but—"

"Adam, pick up your wares and move forward at once, away from the tiller area."

"But why, Captain?"

"I'll explain later when we assemble the crew on deck. As for now, move your men and equipment forward as quickly as possible." John turned back to the gunner. "I can find my own way topside, McCoy. Pass the word to the gunners that the doctor has moved forward."

"Aye, aye, sir!"

John scaled the ladder to the main deck. By now the sun was well into its slow arc skyward, bathing the ship in a sparkle of reflected morning light. Waiting for John on the quarterdeck were his four officers; Ben Gunn, Robert Ormerod, David Noble, and Jack Van Mourik.

"David!" John trotted aft. "Order the men piped to muster!"

Moments later, the shrill tune of the bosun's pipe rang out over the ship, bringing the entire crew to the main deck.

"Attention on deck!" The bosun waited for the chatter to stop. "The captain has a word for you before we go into battle!"

Doctor McKenzie joined the others as John stepped forward. "As I'm sure you all know by now, we'll be engaging *Le Tiburon* in approximately one hour." He pointed south at Puerto Rico. "If we should be sunk—and mind you I believe we will prevail—that is where you will seek refuge."

"Since we carry an enormous treasure, I don't expect either of our enemies to fire at our hull—at least not below the water line. Their strategy will be to disable us by taking off our masts or by damaging our rudder." He looked to the doctor, to see that he understood about the tiller room. Adam nodded that he did. John was satisfied, so he continued.

"Whether or not they're successful in either of these tactics, they'll then attempt to board us. We can expect to lose several men to their cannons and pistol fire, but I've fought *Le Tiburon* before, and I believe with a little Providential help, we'll prevail."

A man called out. "If we sink *Le Tiburon*—what then, Captain?"

"Then we'll need to find a safe place to stop, where we'll attend to our wounded and repair our ship." He waited while the crew cheered. "And now my fellow Americans—to your battle stations! We've a pirate ship to sink!"

☠ ☠ ☠

The sun was high and the watch had just struck four bells when *Le Tiburon* began her attack maneuver. She approached from slightly windward of the

Silver Cloud's wake. Just as John had predicted, the *Eagle* was holding off several leagues to the east.

At two-hundred yards astern, *Le Tiburon* altered course slightly to starboard to cross the *Silver Cloud*'s wake to lee. John turned and called. "Robert! Go to my cabin and supervise those two aft gun crews. I want those pirates kept out of range of our rudder as long as possible!"

Shortly after Robert had dropped from sight, the first of the two stern cannons sent a round of bar stock twirling through *Le Tiburon*'s rigging, leaving a bone-shaped tear in the flying jib and splintering a lower yard as it continued aft through the forest of masts, spars, and lines. The second cannon fired a round shot through the pirate's bow planking and gun deck. But on she came, apparently unconcerned with the damage Robert's two cannons were inflicting upon her.

Robert climbed the ladder enough to report to John. "She didn't return my fire!"

"I noticed! My guess is that Smoot told her captain that we only had those two cannons, and that he can take his time disabling us."

"They've moved forward, out of my two cannon's range! Do you want me to remain with these two cannons or come above deck?"

"Come up but leave word with the two crews to protect the rudder!"

Two minutes later, Robert joined his captain near the aft rail. John was still studying his attacker. By his count there were more than fifty pirates along the rail, and they were all armed with flintlocks, daggers, and cutlasses.

"They're preparing to board us, aren't they?"

John nodded. "The fools want the treasure so bad that they'll commit suicide to get it, and they'll attempt a boarding from our lee, if I allow it!"

"If you allow it?"

"Aye. Their canvas is set for speed, and they'll have to spill half of it to slow for a boarding maneuver."

"And?"

"They'll try to do it, but they won't be able to touch a single line." John turned and pointed into his own sails. "Look! Our best marksmen are in the trees ready to rain down lead on the first man who touches a rope." John watched the pirates closely. "I may be wrong, but it's possible that they believe we are unarmed, except for those two aft cannons."

As *Le Tiburon* began to pass to leeward, a storm of pistol fire rained down onto the deck of the pirates. At the same time, the facades that covered the larboard gun ports were raised and all the cannons began firing at near point-blank range below *Le Tiburon*'s waterline. Just as John had planned, the pirates' greater speed quickly drove her past her prey and into the open water beyond.

John looked up at his rigging. "Mister Noble! Have your sharpshooters take a last shot at them and then have them come down to join the gun crews to starboard! We'll be moving to her lee, and I'll want your best broadside into her stern and up her larboard side!"

"By your order, Captain Jones!" David slung his rifle about his shoulder and slid a sheet to the deck.

John watched for the exact moment and turned to the helmsman. "Now, Poynter! Hard to larboard!" The *Silver Cloud* seemed to bury its bow in the waves for a moment as her forward movement was cut in half and her massive bowsprit swung within twenty yards of *Le Tiburon*'s taffrail. For a moment, the eyes of the two captains met in a defiant stare.

"I'll have that treasure or die tryin', Captain Jones!" Pritchard drew and fired his pistol at the Scotsman. The ball hit the young helmsman in the left thigh, dropping him to the deck.

Captain Jones grabbed the spinning wheel and yelled back a cryptic reply. "Since you know me by name, then you'll remember the *Falmouth Packet* also, and how she took off your rudder near Charles Town two years ago!"

"That was you?"

"Aye, and I'll do worse to you today!" A new helmsman relieved John at the wheel and the injured man was taken below. John turned to his first officer. "We'll serve *Le Tiburon* her second broadside now!"

A moment later, the afternoon sky was filled with white smoke as a wall of iron crashed into and through *Le Tiburon*'s hull. The two massive ships stood no more than a hundred feet apart, making every shot point-blank. But still the pirates sent their cannon shot upward through the *Silver Cloud*'s rigging as Captain Smoot had ordered.

John picked up his speaking trumpet and called forward. "All sheet crews, take up grappling hooks and small arms to starboard, for we've a hand fight before us! And since the cutthroats offered us no quarter, there will be none returned!"

Rather than risk having his helmsman misunderstand his order and turn the wrong way, John took the helm once more. At just the right moment, he threw the *Silver Cloud* hard to starboard, driving her directly into the path of the turning ship. A panic broke out on both ships as the bowsprit of *Le Tiburon* rammed over the *Silver Cloud*'s starboard bulwarks amidships.

There was a tremendous shudder aboard both ships as the figurehead on *Le Tiburon*'s bow shattered against the *Silver Cloud*'s rail. Nearly every man was thrown to the deck as the two entangled ships began to twist counterclockwise in the blue swells. A dozen grappling hooks flew and bit deeply into *Le Tiburon* wherever they could, coupling the two great ships together.

"My God!" Robert was certain John had gone mad. "What on earth have you done? Do you want us to go down with them?" As he spoke the words, a mass of pirates scrambled through their jib stays toward the *Silver Cloud*, and a thunder of small arms fire erupted from the Cloud's deck and crosstrees. Those pirates not killed by the first volley, or by the jabbing pikes, quickly retreated to their own deck.

There was no point in John or the new helmsman staying at the wheel, nor for any of the crew to remain at their sailing stations, for the two ships were locked together like drunken lovers on hell's dance floor. *Le Tiburon* was fastened amidships and perpendicular to the *Silver Cloud*.

"McCoy!"

"Aye, Captain?"

"Can you open their hull enough to fill them with a dose of hot loads and grape shot! I want her set afire, and her planking stripped from her ribs!"

"Aye, Captain!"

One by one the great frigate's cannons belched out their fire and brimstone into the bow and flanks of the helpless pirate ship. Helpless, because none of *Le Tiburon*'s main cannons could be trained forward more than ten degrees beyond the perpendicular. The only firepower she could return was small arms and the three swivel guns mounted on her forward rails.

It was a short and one-sided battle. While the *Silver Cloud*'s center guns punched holes in *Le Tiburon*'s bow and sent a hail of destruction through the length of her gun deck, the remaining guns raked the pirate ship at her waterline. As the two great ships twisted in their grisly dance of death, the breeze began to carry away the accumulation of sulfurous smoke, revealing to the *Silver Cloud*'s crew the destruction they had wrought on their enemy.

Like the executioner who tore the flesh from the old Baptist preacher's spine and ribs in Culpeper, the *Silver Cloud*'s gunners peeled *Le Tiburon*'s planking away piece by piece. Between each explosion of cannon and shattering of wood, the screams of pirates could be heard as they were either thrown or leaped from the holes opened along her waterline. Just as John had ordered, cannons four through seven were loaded with a combination of bar stock and what McCoy called a hot load—pieces of burning oak and coal. Two of the loads hit their mark, causing several secondary explosions within the pirate's hull.

Only the more seasoned sailors aboard the *Silver Cloud* had ever witnessed such human carnage. One of *Le Tiburon*'s powder monkeys—a lad no more than ten or twelve years old—jumped from the inferno that his ship's gun deck had become. It was to quench his burning clothes that he leaped, completely unaware that his left arm and part of his shoulder had been ripped away in the battle. Another pirate stood in one of the yawning holes on the windward side, holding his face. Then he dropped his hands to his sides, revealing that his jaw was missing. He stood for a moment longer, then toppled forward into the sea.

By now, the dark waters were quickly spilling into *Le Tiburon*'s stern. As her bow rose, John gave the order to cut the grappling lines to send her backward to wallow helplessly among the oncoming swells.

"McCoy! I want her finished!"

"John!" Robert grabbed him by his sword arm. "They've had enough!"

"Not until they're sunk and every last one of them is dead!" John pried the hand from his arm.

"But look at them, John. They're finished already. It's time to show some mercy?"

"It's justice, Robert, not mercy they've earned! If the tables were turned, do you suppose for an instant they would treat us otherwise?"

CHAPTER TWELVE:
Casks of Poisoned Rum

The warm waters of the Caribbean teem with sharks. At feeding time, these mindless wolves of the sea are drawn to their prey by not only the smell of blood but by low-frequency sound waves pulsating for long distances through the ocean. While the one-sided battle raged between the two great ships, each crash of ball into and through the inner members of *Le Tiburon*'s hull, and each thud and bump of her stores colliding with her bulkheads, sent out that unmistakable call to feeding time. And long before the last grappling hook had been severed and the great bowsprit had ripped itself loose from the *Silver Cloud*'s deck and lower rigging, the sea churned with the frenzied, gray beasts.

The cannon fire had finished its ugly work, turning over the task of sinking *Le Tiburon* to her own ballast—the tons of stones placed years before in her bilges for vertical stability. She was sinking rapidly now, slipping backwards below the swells more quickly with each passing wave. The thick smoke that had been pouring from her hatches and lee side ceased abruptly with a hiss and the cloud of white steam, indicating that the sea had reached the seat of the flames. She was a dying beast, crying out her agony in tremendous groans and heaving sighs as one after another compartment flooded and filled from stern to bow. As her ballast continued to pull her down, she pitched backwards until her mainmast lay back flat on the sea and the bowsprit pointed skyward in a final salute to her defeat.

And then, with a final burst of air and smoke through the churning water, it was over. The bone-chilling sounds of sucking and blowing had finally stopped, and her figurehead and bowsprit descended from view, leaving only the scattered flotsam as mute testimony that a ship had once been there. But there were also the seven pirates clinging to the splintered planking, broken pieces of rail, and canvas-tangled yardarms+.

David pointed at the men crying for mercy. "What about them, John? Shall I order the boats out?"

John shook his head. "There won't be time!" While the two watched, the sharks circled closer to their prey. "But I guess decency demands that we do something for them."

"Time?" David could not believe his ears. "I don't understand!" David fell silent when he realized that the survivor's calls for help had changed to screams of terror. Up until *Le Tiburon* had sunk, the sharks had remained at a distance, as if the great ship were a competitor for the meal they had come to take. But with its descent into the depths, the sharks closed in. The first three to venture close to the men were small, only six to eight feet long. The fourth shark was a giant—a great white. Its slate-gray pectoral fin stood two feet out of the water as it cruised straight for the three men clinging to a length of top rail.

Before the great shark had made its attack, one of the dead pirates, who had been cut in half and thrown into the sea by an explosion, suddenly popped to the surface, twitching, and jerking about as if resurrected and was back to cast a final curse upon its enemy. As the pale face turned about for a lifeless gaze at the *Silver Cloud*, three large barracudas thrashed about at the surface while they played a grizzly game of tug-of-war for the flesh of the pirate's arms and ribs.

"Help us, mates!" It was one of the pirates. "Don't let us die like this! Don't let the sharks…" He fell silent to watch the large fin pass close abeam and then twist about toward him and his mate. There was a flash of white underbelly as the monster rolled onto its back.

It is claimed by some that what is in a man's heart will come out just before he goes to meet his Maker. If that is true, then this pirate was a Godly man, for his last words—the words spoken just before the great shark fastened upon his thorax with its multiple rows of teeth—were the words of a Baptist preacher.

"Oh, sweet Jesus! Have mercy on this poor sinner!" Then he was gone.

A deathly quiet fell over the *Silver Cloud* and the six remaining pirates while they stared at the spot on the splintered yard where the man had clung moments before.

David pointed at one of the ship's boats. "Shall I order the boat lowered?"

"There's no point." Two more of the pirates were pulled from the flotsam amidst screams and boiling water that suddenly turned crimson with their blood. "Even if they deserved the least mercy, those sharks will finish their task long before we can begin ours."

"Our captain is right, David." Robert was as shocked by the spectacle as the young Jamaican, but this was not the first time he had seen such carnage. He turned to John. "But David's right, too. We can't let them die that way."

"No, I suppose we can't." John turned. "David, I want four of our best marksmen to the rail with their rifles."

"But there are too many of them!"

"They won't be shooting at the sharks."

"You're going to shoot the men, rather than try to save them?"

"I have no choice, David, unless you want those poor souls to die like their mates."

The four riflemen stepped to the rail as ordered, and at their captain's signal, fired at the four pirates. David turned away in horror when the four balls struck their marks.

The battle was over, with only two of the *Silver Cloud*'s crew dead and three others injured. While the seabirds were fast at work cleaning up after their larger cousins' furious lunch, John walked to the starboard rail where his young friend was retching.

"I'm sorry I had to do that, David. The sharks gave me no choice."

"Don't you think I know that?" David wiped his sleeve across his mouth and turned. "It's just that…" He gave an involuntary shudder. "How can anybody get over this carnage?"

"You're right, David." Robert stepped to the two. "This is exactly why I made that vow at my wedding ceremony. Moira and I witnessed tenfold what you saw here today. All we can do is put it behind us and continue with our mission."

Within twenty minutes the damaged rigging had been cut away and the salvageable lines and sailcloth stowed. Following a quick look at his chart, John set a course for Boca Del Cibuco where they anchored in deep water a hundred yards outside the surf line.

While the sun neared the western horizon, they had nearly completed the removal of the damaged and useless rigging while saving the portions that could be salvaged. Still playing their part, the *Eagle* sailed to a position a hundred yards seaward—between the *Silver Cloud* and the *Remora*.

"Ahoy *Eagle*!" Captain Jones held the bullhorn to his mouth. "Send across your first officer for a parley!"

"Morgan!"

"I heard, Captain." The lad looked across at the *Silver Cloud*. "They'll be wanting to know why we were not there to protect them from *Le Tiburon*."

"Bring me Cutter and two of his best men." A few minutes later, Danny Cutter stood before Captain Smoot with two of his mates. "They want a parley, and Captain Jones is going to want to know why we were not there when they were attacked. Can you tell them a believable story?"

"Aye, Captain."

Twenty minutes later, the three men approached the larger ship. "Ahoy, *Silver Cloud*!" John stepped to the rail. "Captain Steele sends his apologies for not being here to protect you from *Le Tiburon*'s attack!"

"Why wasn't the *Eagle* there?"

"None of us knew you were gone until first light. As we were getting underway, *Le Tiburon* came around Cotton Garden Point and attacked us with several hits to our rigging. It took us several hours to repair and replace what was damaged."

"Captain Jones!" It was one of the other men. "Did any of the pirates survive?"

"No, and those who survived our guns were eaten by the sharks."

"What about Captain Smoot? Did he go down with the rest?"

"Aye, along with every last one of them!" John pointed north to where the *Remora* was tacking back several leagues to the north. "I want you to tell Captain Steele to anchor a hundred yards seaward and keep an eye on the *Remora*!"

"Who are they, Captain Jones?"

"I have to assume that they are pirates, but they have held their distance so far."

"Aye! We'll tell Captain Steele!"

"Also tell him that I will come across tomorrow morning for a parley!" John paused. "How are your supplies holding up? Is there anything you need from me?"

Uh…" The three had a quick discussion. "We've run out of rum. Might you be able to spare us a few casks?"

"Let me check!" John turned to Adam. "Do you have anything in your medical supplies that we can put in the rum to put the *Eagle* crew to sleep?"

"What do you have in mind, Captain Jones?

"I'm going to take a couple dozen of our Indian fighters for a swim tonight."

"I'm certain I do." The doctor turned and left.

John turned and called down to the men. "We've enough to share. How many ten-gallon casks can you carry in your boat?"

"Four, if you can spare them!"

"Hold while we make a count!" Twenty minutes later, the four casks were lowered into the *Eagle*'s boat. "Don't drink too much of that tonight because you still have to protect us from the *Remora* if they should attack."

"Aye, aye, Captain Jones, and thank you !"

"Well?" John turned to Adam. "Did you find anything useful?"

"Each of those casks has two pints of laudanum mixed in—more than enough to put every man to sleep after just half a pint."

"Considering how long it will take to affect them, what time would you suggest we go for our swim?"

"They'll start drinking the rum as soon as they get it aboard." Adam looked to the setting sun. "I'd say that before you can get the raiding team together and briefed, every man on the *Eagle* will be fast asleep."

☠ ☠ ☠

"Listen up!" Joshua reached down and touched one of the four casks. "Since Captain Jones still believes that we are the *Silver Cloud*'s protector, only one of these four will be opened tonight!" This brought a rumble of complaints from assembled crew. "Do any of you know how many pints are in ten gallons?"

"One of the men held up his cup and called out. "I know my sums, Captain! There are eighty, so that means each of us gets almost a pint and a half!"

"Then I want you to step up here and ration this out—a pint to each man."

"Aye, Captain."

"Wait!" Henry held up three cups while the crew formed a queue. "You want me to get our share before it's gone, Captain?"

"No, we've still got that bottle David Noble brought across yesterday, along with those three Cuban cigars." He pointed aft at the companionway. "Let's go down to my cabin and enjoy the evening away from all that noise."

A moment later, first rations were doled out and the men began singing the words to an old pirate ballad that had been sung by seamen for two decades. As the rum took effect, the words began to slur. "Through winds of treachery a bloody tale's told, of Captain Rip Rap and Porto Bello Gold. How he left Flint an' Silver on Spyglass to wait, while he took Saint Trinidad's pieces of eight. Buckets of blood were spilled in the hold, Flint accused Rip Rap, 'The treasure ye've stole. Ye took it to the Island called Dead Man's Chest, where ye laid it by fer half a scores rest.' Flint killed Rip Rap an' on Spyglass did hide, o'er half a million where six men died. Bones took the map an' to Bristol did run, an' left Flint's bones to bleach in the sun. A curse on the jewels, the pearls, and the gold, a curse on the pirates what's honor was sold. A curse on the Yorkman what refuses to tell, of the treasure laid by—may he rot in hell. Fifteen men on the Dead Man's Chest, Yo-ho-ho, and a bottle of rum. Drink and the devil had done for the rest. Yo-ho-ho, and a bottle of rum."

By the time the drunken pirates had finished the song and its choruses for a third time, the laudanum had done its work. Some of the pirates were able to get to their hammocks before sleep overtook them, but most of the crew fell asleep where they sang.

Once in the captain's cabin, Henry pried out the cork and filled their three glasses. Joshua handed out the cigars and lit a candle from the lantern. Henry watched with interest while Joshua bit the ends from his cigar.

"Is this your first cigar, Henry?"

"I hate to admit it, Captain, but I've never had the occasion before tonight."

"Well, watch what Alan and I do, and then copy us." Joshua leaned to the candle and puffed his cigar alive.

A moment later, the lad broke into a coughing fit as the acrid smoke filled his lungs. "Ah!" He finally caught his breath. "Now I'm glad I never did this before."

"You're not supposed to fill your lungs, Henry, just your mouth. Then you blow it out like this." Alan blew a perfect smoke ring at the lad.

"Well, one of you could have warned me."

Alan turned to Joshua. "I hear that Captain Jones is coming aboard in the morning."

"Aye." Joshua tried to blow a ring but failed. "I expect he'll be telling us what he intends to do between here and Kings Town."

"So, you'll need me." He held up his glass of rum. "It's a good thing you've kept me alive this long, isn't it?"

"I told you that when I get the treasure, I'll release you so that you could go back to Christiansted to free your crew." Joshua took a puff and tried another smoke ring. "Are you saying that you don't trust me?"

"How can I trust anything you say after what you did to Nate Pritchard and his crew?"

"I sent them to disable the *Silver Cloud*, and they failed. That was on them, not me."

"But you told Pritchard that the *Silver Cloud* only had two cannons and that they were both left on that cliff."

Joshua jumped to his feet. "Are you calling me a liar?"

"Liars are, as liars do!"

"Arm yourself, Captain Steele, and follow me up to the deck where we'll settle this, like men!" Joshua threw down his cigar, took a sword from the bulkhead, and marched from the cabin.

"Why'd you do that, Captain Steele?" Henry watched while Alan took down the other sword. "If we're going to get that treasure, we're going to need both of you alive and well all the way to Kings Town."

"It's a matter of honor, Henry, and the treasure be damned."

By the time Joshua emerged onto the deck, John's raiding party had already found the entire crew asleep and had applied transom knots to their wrists and ankles. The two dozen men now stood amidship silhouetted against the two lanterns at the bow.

"Captain!" Henry followed Alan topside and held up the bottle. "There's one more round of rum in the bottle! Why don't we put down our swords and finish our party?"

"Because he called me a liar." He pointed his sword at Alan. "On guard!"

As the two advanced upon one another with swords held at the ready, Henry stepped past them toward the group of men. "Captain, I think the men want you to open another cask of rum."

"What?" Smoot turned. "Is that true? You want more rum?" Nobody answered him, so he raised his hand to block the light. "What's going on?"

"We're taking the *Eagle* from you."

"This is rich!" Steele gave a laugh and pointed at the gathered men. "Your men found out that you lied to Pritchard, and now they don't trust you any more than I do!"

"So, it's a mutiny, is it?" Smoot waved the sword in their faces. When they did not retreat, he slashed at the two nearest men. "You fools! I told you we would wait and take the treasure after it reaches Kings Town!" He waited for one of the men to answer but none did. "If this is a mutiny, then whoever's leading you needs to stand forward and be man enough to fight me for the ship!" There was still no answer. "Very well. If you intend to cut me down, then do me the decency of letting me choose who I fight first, like is fitting for pirates." He pointed at the man in the center. "You! What's your name so I know who I've killed?"

"I'm John Paul Jones, the man who crippled *Le Tiburon* with a single cannon shot off the coast of Savannah."

"Yes!" Alan put the tip of his sword at Joshua's back and pressed it through his shirt until a trail of blood showed itself. "You're now my prisoner, Joshua Smoot, so either yield to Captain Jones this instant or I will run you through like you threatened to do to one of my young men back at Christiansted."

"Belay!" Joshua sucked a gasp through his clenched teeth and let his sword swing loose on his thumb. "I wouldn't have killed the lad, Alan."

"Another lie?"

"What did you put in their rum, Captain Jones?" Alan stepped around and faced Joshua.

"It was laudanum—probably more than necessary."

"That's how Smoot took the *Eagle*." He turned to the pirate. "They call it poetic justice, Joshua, so you have this coming."

"Wait!" Robert stepped to the three. "You keep calling him Joshua Smoot." He pointed north. "That's John Manley—the man Long John Silver sent to New York to buy my mark on his map!" He pointed at Henry. "And that's the message boy who took my daughter and held her hostage!"

"We didn't mean to kill her, Robert."

"Do you have any idea how seeing our burned daughter dropped in the middle of the roadway tore at our souls?"

"You must have had another enemy, Robert—somebody who took revenge by distracted Henry with a prostitute long enough to set that fire." Joshua stepped to the Yorkman. "So, now that you've finally caught up with Morgan and me, what do you intend?"

"I intend to kill you both." Robert raised his sword and looked to his captain. "Do I have your permission, John?"

Smoot's eyes flashed fear and hatred as he retreated a step.

"Belay, Robert." John stepped between the two and applied a constrictor knot to the pirate's wrists. These two and the saboteur will be tried at an Admiralty Court and executed."

"You're willing to let Jones do that to me, Robert?" Joshua studied the Yorkman for a long moment. "Henry and I killed your little girl, and now you're willing to let a bunch of men in white wigs exact your revenge?"

"You didn't kill Jane."

"But she…" Henry stepped forward and held out his roped arms as if he was carrying the dead girl's burned body. "I laid Jane's burned body in the street with everybody watching. You and your wife knelt in the street over her." Henry shook his head. "I know a dead body when I see it."

"That wasn't our daughter you laid in the street."

"I don't understand, Robert." Joshua looked to Henry and back to the Yorkman. "We all saw her burned body. Those were the ropes we tied to her wrists and ankles. That was her dress."

"A man brought our Jane home to us later that same day—safe and sound."

"What man?"

"The old pirate who sent you with the bribe money—Captain Long John Silver."

CHAPTER THIRTEEN:
When The Silver Clouds Meet

While Joshua and Henry were loaded onto the *Eagle*'s boat for transit to the *Silver Cloud*, Robert stepped to the two captains. "Gentlemen, we have a problem that jeopardizes our mission—something that must be dealt with immediately, one way or another."

"Oh?" John slid his sword through his belt. "Captain Steele has his ship back, and the pirates are subdued. What else has gone wrong?"

"Doctor McKinsey told me that the laudanum will wear off and the men will begin waking at dawn, and we've nearly fifty prisoners below that will be waking in a couple hours." He pointed at the *Silver Cloud*. "Correct me if I'm wrong, but our brig can only hold a few men—no more than a half dozen at most."

"Robert is right, John. Those men are going to be a millstone around your necks if you take them aboard the treasure ship."

"Then…" John looked to his ship and back to the two. "What do you suggest, Robert?"

"Our mission is to get General Washington's cannons to Charles Town as quickly as possible."

"I see it, Captain Jones." Alan paused for a breath. "Since we three agree that they cannot be taken aboard the *Silver Cloud*, then we have only two choices."

"Are you suggesting that we execute them?"

"It's either that—that we do it now, before they begin to wake—or we boat them to shore before they start untying each other."

"Aye." It took John only a moment. "Order the boats out. We're releasing them to Puerto Rico."

The transfer of the forty-seven pirates to shore took just under two hours. When the last six men were laid on the sand, Alan stepped to John.

"Have you had an opportunity to consider me request?"

"Yes, Alan. Since we need to be underway by noon, I'll need a list of the crewmen and supplies you need, as quickly as you can put it together."

"I've already made them up. There are more than enough men who have volunteered to help. All I needed was your approval." He pulled a folded paper from his pocket and handed it to the younger man. "Those are the names of the ten seamen to man the rigging, along with the provisions we'll need. I'll trust you to select the additional dozen fighters." He looked back to the *Eagle*. "Once I get the provisions and men aboard, I'll be ready to leave with you and the *Remora*."

"You can see Robert about the provisions, and I'll pass the word for the men to transfer their gear."

As planned, the *Eagle* sailed east toward Saint Croix while the *Silver Cloud* and the *Remora* sailed west. Three days later at mid-afternoon, the treasure ship's massive anchor splashed into the turquoise waters between Little and Great Inagua Islands. As the bubbles spread out on the surface and then cleared away in a circle of light foam, the enormous iron and oak hook struck a coral head and settled into the white sand. The chain was allowed to slack another twenty-five yards before it was stopped and the shackle was driven through the enormous link. The great anchor rose on its side for a moment while one of the large flukes drove itself deep into the sandy bottom. The *Silver Cloud's* twin lay anchored two hundred yards to the south and was already lowering a boat. According to John Silver's order, the *Remora* remained under full sail a league to windward, just in case any other ship tried to approach. John ordered all boats lowered and the crew to make ready to begin moving across once the two cargoes were confirmed.

John watched the activity at the other *Silver Cloud*. "It appears they're more anxious than we are to trade ships and get underway."

"Captain." David handed John the sheets of paper. "Robert and I have finished our inventory of the treasure, and Ben Gunn was right. As you can see, that chest of jewels with the King's crown was extra."

"The crew will be pleased."

"Yes." David looked to the men lowering the boats. "We've already transferred it into two duffel bags, so with your permission, I'll send it across in the first boat."

"Not until we inspect and count the cannons." John looked at the papers. "I'll give this to Captain Silver when he arrives."

"Robert and I will be waiting for him at the lazarette so he can confirm our count."

"No." John shook his head. "We can't risk allowing those two together again. Robert will kill him this time for certain."

"Then…"

"We'll wait until John Silver comes across. Once you have him taken aside, I'll take Robert across with me to count the cannons"

As they spoke, a man with a Jamaican accent called from the gunship's first boat. "Ahoy, *Silver Cloud*! Do you have a young man named David Noble aboard?"

"Father!" David ran to the rail and looked down. "What are you doing here?"

"I'm here to count the treasure!" A moment later, Charles Noble's boat was secured to the ladder, and he climbed up to the main deck.

"Welcome aboard, Mister Noble!" John extended a hand of greeting. "This is a pleasant surprise, especially for your son! We expected John Silver to be coming across again."

Charles looked back at the cannon ship. "Again?"

"He didn't tell you about our meeting before we took on water at the Luquillo River?"

"No, but my brother keeps a lot of things from me." Charles gave his son a hug. "He did tell me about Mister Ormerod trying to kill him but didn't say when that happened."

"We'd assumed Silver would want to count the treasure personally, but after that confrontation the other day, I cannot allow him and Robert to be on the same ship again."

"That's why he sent me across in his place?" Charles looked about the main deck. "Shall we be at it?"

John nodded. "Your son assures me that everything's ready for you, Mister Noble."

"Will David be helping me?"

"Of course."

"Thank you, Captain Jones!" David grabbed his father's arm and escorted him to the ladder. "This is wonderful, Father! We'll have time to talk before you have to leave again."

John called after the two. "Watch for my signal David, before you start sending the crew across."

With a curt salute from David, John climbed down into the boat where Ben Gunn was waiting.

David led the way down to the officer's companionway but stopped and turned to his father. "I've missed you so much, Father. I wish there were a way you could continue with us to Charles Town."

Charles gave his son a broad smile. "Well, David, the good Lord has indeed smiled on both of us this day."

"You're coming with us?" David paused. "I thought you'd be returning to oversee the unloading of the treasure at Jamaica. What if he—"

"I've already discussed that with your uncle. I think after all these years I can trust my own brother."

☠ ☠ ☠

While John and Ben climbed the ladder and stepped through the opening in the larboard gunwale of the cannon ship, Captain Silver stepped forward with an elderly woman on his arm. "Welcome aboard, gentlemen!" He gave his wife a smile. "You already know my wife, Captain Jones, but Ben has never met her."

John gave her a salute. "Yes—and nobody makes a better lamb stew than you, Misses Silver."

"Please, Captain Jones. Call me Betty."

"Betty it is, and you may call me John"

"Well, well!" John Silver grabbed Ben and gave him a hug. "If it isn't my old mate, Ben Gunn!"

"Top o' the day to ya, Captain Silver!"

Silver released the old man, stepped back, and looked down at his legs. "You're looking a far sight better than when they were burning your legs on Dead Man's Chest."

Silver stepped back and looked down. The old man's dressings had been removed, exposing the neat row of diamond-shaped cauterizing burns that ran up the outside of each calf from ankle to knee. "Are they healing well?"

"They still sting a bit when I sweat, but other than that, I'm doing fine."

Ben noticed his captain looking at his calves. Ben twisted his right leg outward toward the younger man. "Sort of fashionable, isn't it, Cap'n Jones?"

"That wasn't the word I was going to use, Ben."

"They're the perfect scars fer a storyteller, says I." The old man turned back to Silver. "When they were burning me for the location of the treasure, I had a dream that you were there."

"Aye, that was no dream, Ben. We saw what they were doing to you and came ashore in the dark." He held up his hands. "I killed two of the nine black-hearts with my own hands."

"Ben and I appreciate what you did for him, Captain Silver, but could we get to the business at hand?"

"What's the rush? Ben and I've not seen each other for years—not since he released me from the *Hispaniola* when we were anchored at Puerto Plata. That deserves a minute or two, doesn't it?"

"Yes, but you and he can reminisce while I count the cannons, can't you?"

"Aye, that we can!" The old pirate pushed himself away from the pin rail and turned to his wife. "This shouldn't take us too long. When we're finished, you and I will boat across to the treasure ship."

Ten minutes later, John and Ben descended the first ladder to the gun deck—stopping occasionally to allow the old pirate to catch up. At the gun deck, Silver pointed at the row of new carronades at the disguised gun ports. "Ha! Reminds me of those pictures they showed us in church of how the Papists lined up the Baptists for torture!" The old pirate pointed to the ladder. "Let's continue to the bilges, so you can count the rest of your cannons."

The three descended to the crew birthing deck and then down through to ship's stores to the bilges. The cannons lay in neat rows with the carriages and supporting equipment stacked to the side. All the ballast stones had been removed so the cannons were fully exposed.

"There they are, Captain Jones, like promised."

John stepped out onto the cannons and began counting.

Silver gave a clap of his large hands and a laugh. "As you can see, the tools and carriages are there too, just as Mister Jefferson ordered."

Ben stepped out and stood with a foot on each of two cannons and looked about. "There's no way that we can unstack them to make a full count, Cap'n Jones, but from the looks of it, the number is most likely close to correct." Ben turned and gave Silver a suspicious look. "Can Captain Jones trust you that they're all here?"

"You pain me to me marrow Ben, by suggesting that I would lie to you. Wasn't it me that helped you escape from the *Walrus* in Savannah when Billy Bones was set to kill Robert, Moira, and you?"

"Aye?"

"Then, by the powers! If you can't trust old Long John Silver when he gives his word, then you cannot trust Charlie Noble either!"

"We can trust David's father, Ben. If Charles says all the cannons, carriages, and support equipment are here, that's good enough for me."

As Ben spoke, a young man stepped from the shadows and walked to the three. "Greetings, gentlemen."

"Ah! General Washington's Aide-De-Camp. He has been with the cannons for over a year—from the day they were loaded onto *Amazing Grace* at Falkirk—to now."

You and Captain Jones haven't seen each other for over a year—not since he was sent to Falkirk to see to the loading of General Washington's cannons."

"That's right." Silver stepped to the man. "His real name is Joseph Reed—

John took the man's hand. "It's good to see you again, Joseph. I trust Captain Silver and his brother have treated you well?"

"Very well, but I am anxious to finally return to Charles Town."

"Say!" Silver pointed east. "I hear that you sent a raiding party across and liberated the *Eagle.*"

"Three of them came across to us on their boat, and we sent them back with several casks of rum filled with laudanum. When we climbed aboard, the whole crew was drunk and confused."

"What happened to Joshua Smoot and Henry Morgan? Did you kill them with the rest?"

"Smoot and Morgan lie in chains in our brig with the saboteur. Since we had no room for the rest, we put them ashore before they woke up."

"You took Smoot alive?"

"He surrendered his sword to me on the deck of the *Eagle.*"

"Never!" The old man raised a fist at John. "Joshua Smoot would never surrender his sword! Gentlemen do a fool thing like that—not men of Smoot's cut!"

"It was that, or Captain Steele was to run him through."

"And what might you be planning to do with the two—Smoot and Morgan?" He touched his throat. "Are they to dance at the gallows? "

"They'll both stand before an Admiralty court for their crimes of piracy."

"Captain Silver!" One of the crew called from the ladder above. "Your brother is coming back from the treasure ship!"

"Well, mates, what say we go topside and hear what Charlie has to report?" When Silver finally reached the main deck, Charles' and David's boat was tying up to the side. He walked across the deck and looked down at his brother. "Is it all there, Charlie?"

"Every farthing, just as you told me it would be."

"And that chest of jewels with the King's crown in it?" Silver licked his lips and gave Ben a questioning look. "Is it there too?"

"I can answer that, Captain Silver."

Silver looked about at John. He didn't like the young man's tone.

"Our bargain was the thousand cannons for a million and a half worth of treasure. That is exactly what we are leaving on the treasure ship. That chest of jewels is excess, and we're keeping it to split with our crew."

"Like hell you are!" Silver's eyes burned with fire. "One word from me and my men will scuttle this ship and send the cannons to the bottom with her!

Your precious cannons and the future of the American colonies will sink beyond salvage!"

"No, you won't!" It was Charles. "We made an agreement with them, and they've fulfilled their part to the letter!" Charles placed himself between the two captains. "They've delivered the agreed amount, and I'm satisfied!" He turned to John. "When can we begin exchanging crews?"

"Wait!" Silver's tone had softened. "I'll agree to hold to the bargain, but there's one minor concession I'd ask of you, Captain Jones, just to compensate me."

"And what might that be?"

"It's something without value to you but with great value to me."

"What is it, Mister Silver?"

"I want Joshua Smoot and the lad, Henry Morgan left in the brig."

"I already told you that they're to be taken to Charles Town, tried, and hanged."

Silver nodded. "There's no question those two have earned a date with the hangman, but those two have a sentimental value to me."

"I will not release him just to satisfy an old man's sentimentalities. You have fulfilled your side of the agreement and I have fulfilled mine. Smoot and Morgan have earned themselves the gallows."

"Wait." Charles turned to John. "Is it so important that Smoot and Morgan be hanged? Isn't it your mission to ensure that the cannons reach Charles Town?"

Silver looked at John for a long moment, and then spoke the words slowly. "Please, Captain Jones. Grant an old man this one request."

"Very well. Smoot and Morgan will remain in the brig."

The old pirate smiled and clapped his hands. "Then it's settled!"

John turned to his first officer. "Give the signal to begin the transfer, David. I want to be under sail before dark."

CHAPTER FOURTEEN:
Cannons to Charles Town

Joshua Smoot and Henry Morgan had been in the brig for three days and nights when Silver finally ordered their release. The bright sunlight nearly blinded them as their weak legs carried them onto the main deck. They stood for a long moment shading their eyes while they gained their bearings.

"Welcome back from the gates of hell, mates!" John Silver walked aft and stopped face to face with Smoot. Do you two brig rats remember me?"

"Of course, we do. You're Jack Bridger." Joshua shaded his eyes against the bright sun. "What is all this talk Henry and I have been hearing that Long John Silver finally got his treasure?"

"Why would that surprise you, considering your treachery against the old pirate?"

"My treachery?"

"That the map you brought back from New York sent the old pirate on a fool's errand? He wasted a full month sailing to and from Dead Man's Chest, and there was no treasure."

"Ormerod had signed and dated the map, and was ready to make the mark, but that's when Henry brought their daughter's chard body and laid it in the street in front of us."

"Then…"

"I made that mark on John Silver's map."

"Oh?"

"I had to or he would not have given me the location of John Flint's body."

"And what did you do with his body when you found it?"

"I sat on the rotting *Walrus* and watching the carrion pick his bones clean on the mud flats."

"Did you, indeed?"

"You don't believe me?"

"Oh, I believe you stood guard over a rotted body, but the bones that remained were not the bones of John Flint."

"He told you that his map was a lie?"

"Aye, and I have a confession to make to you."

"I'm not a Papist priest but I'm listening."

"I know the map John Silver gave you was a lie because I was there on the *Walrus* when John Flint died of rum poisoning. I watched our sailmakers sew his body and two ballast stones up in sail cloth, and I helped dump him from the *Walrus* into the Savannah River."

"Then who's body did I dig up?"

"You kept watch on a stranger's body while John Silver dug dry holes on Dead Man's Chest." The two stared at each other for several moments. Finally, Silver smiled. "The devil's right, Joshua. You and Long John Silver deserve each other and the lies you traded."

Joshua looked about the deck. "I was told that Long John Silver is aboard, and that it was him who negotiated for Morgan's and my lives. Where is the old devil?"

John Silver spread his arms again. "You don't see him yet, Joshua?"

"I would if I knew what he looked like." Joshua finally realized the obvious. "It's you! You're Long John Silver!"

Henry Morgan stepped forward and pointed at the old man. "I knew that was you in Kings Town when we made that deal about the treasure map !"

Silver turned on the lad. "You did not, Henry, no more than Joshua did."

"But—"

Joshua pointed down at Silver's left leg. "Ormerod asked me about John Silver—if he was the one who sent us. He asked about a wooden left leg."

Silver raised the articulated leg. "I couldn't let you know it was me because Ormerod would never agree to be in league with the likes of Long John Silver." Silver paused. "Don't feel bad, Joshua. I've been Jack Bridger for all these years—ever since the King put a price on my head. If the King's men didn't know who I was, how could you expect to see through my disguise?"

"Do you remember me taking your ring that first day we met—how I took it to the back room to get my magnifier?"

"Yes."

"Are you certain it was your mother's stick pin?"

"Yes!" Joshua gave Silver a questioning look. "Why do you care?"

The old man gave a nod. "I did some research, Joshua, and discovered that you may not be one of John Flint's bastards."

"I've heard the same story from my sister."

"Oh?"

"She told me that I am the son of David and Elaine MacBride, the Marquess and Marchioness of Earlshall Castle at Edinburgh—that it was all in a journal that her mother hid away." Joshua shook his head. "But Sarah has searched and could never find the journal."

"Damn!" Silver gave a frustrated grunt. "And here I did all that research and it's all just hearsay."

☠ ☠ ☠

Within an hour, Captain Jones ordered the cannon ships anchor weighed and set sail for the Charles Town. It was his plan to utilize the shallows as much as possible until they reached the relative safety of the coast of Spanish Florida. This would give him the option, if they were attacked and the ship was sinking, to run her aground or let her slip to the bottom at a depth at which the cannons could be retrieved.

By dusk the next day, the cannon ship had reached Biscayne Bay and altered course to parallel the coastline, just as they had done during their passage through the Bahamas. Four days later, the familiar coastline of South Carolina began to pass abeam.

The *Silver Cloud* was still several leagues short of her destination when two merchantmen flying British colors took up an intercept course. Maneuver as he did, Captain Jones could not avoid an encounter.

He turned to his first officer. "I know they are only merchantmen, but their persistence bothers me, David. Order the guns manned."

"But shouldn't we—" Before David could make his suggestion, the lead ship hoisted a string of banners identifying itself as belonging to Alexander Forrestal.

John gave a laugh of relief. "Well, I'll be. It looks as though our benefactor has arranged a welcoming party for us."

Two glasses later, a long boat pulled across to the *Silver Cloud* with a written message.

Dear Captain Jones:

Given that you are reading this letter, you have returned with the prize. These two merchantmen will provide the distraction you may need to get past the blockade at the mouth of our fine harbor. I look forward to your soon arrival.

With sincere and humble appreciation, I remain,

A. Forrestal

The top watch called down to the helm. "Charles Town, one point off the larboard bow!"

By now, every man aboard—including the officers—was suffering from what sailors call channel fever—that restlessness that always sets in during the last few days before a long journey's end. They all had pooled their money to bet on the day and hour they would first spot their destination. The one hundred forty pounds went to one of the surgeon's mates, but nobody really cared who won—their greatest reward was to finally reach home. It was as if the Lord Himself had reached down and touched the crew the moment the familiar coastline and Fort Sullivan was first spotted, for every man's spirit seemed to come alive at the same moment. Within six hours, their feet would once again touch America's soil and their arms would hold their loved ones.

Shortly after noon, the *Silver Cloud* rounded close abeam Morris Island, and trimmed for the larboard reach to the Forrestal yards on the north shore of Charles Town. The two British naval ships protecting the harbor were completely engaged by Forrestal's decoys, allowing the disguised frigate to slip past, unmolested. Several small fishing boats returning from the open sea joined the *Silver Cloud* on her larboard reach across the harbor toward her berth, creating a small parade for the returning ship.

CHAPTER FIFTEEN:
A Widow's Last Wish

*L*ong John Silver stepped to the helmsman and gave the man a nod. "That went better than I thought it would, Donny."

"Aye, Captain Silver." The man watched the cannon ship weigh anchor and spread her sails. "What are your orders for me and the crew?"

"I want to hold at anchor until the other *Silver Cloud* is a league away, and then we'll sail south."

"But you told us that we're sailing to Savannah, sir. Have you changed your mind?"

"No, I haven't."

"Then, we're going back to Kings Town because you forgot something there?"

"I know this is confusing, Donny, but you don't understand our situation."

"We have the treasure, and we have Captain Smoot aboard. He owns Savannah, so why aren't we sailing north?"

"We are sailing to Savannah." He pointed at the departing ship. "There are over a hundred men aboard that other *Silver Cloud*, and they all want the treasure we carry. I want them to think that we are taking it back to Kings Town."

"Ah!" Donny gave a nod. "As long as the treasure is aboard, there will be men who will do whatever they have to in order to take it from us."

After an hour, the top watch called down. "On deck! The cannon ship is over the horizon!"

John Silver called to his bosun. "Make ready to come about, Grady!" Within twenty minutes, the treasure ship was sailing before the southeasterly toward the Florida coast—the same route as her twin.

"Do you think we fooled them, Captain?"

"Oh, you can count on it, Donny."

"Why isn't Captain Smoot up here with you?"

"He's well enough in body, but his soul is in torment because he lost his ship, his men, and the treasure."

Just then, Henry Morgan came topside. He shaded his eyes for a moment before spotting John Silver. "So, where are we headed, Cap'n Silver?"

"To Savannah."

"A question, Cap'n." Henry joined Silver at the helm. "Judas Pottersfield, huh? Where did you come up with that name?"

"Matthew gave me that name."

"Matthew, the gunner's mate?"

"No, Matthew from the Bible." Both Donny and Henry gave Silver a questioning look. "Judas Iscariot was paid thirty pieces of silver by the priests to betray Jesus with a kiss. Judas felt so much shame afterwards that he threw the money down at the priest's feet and then hung himself. The priests didn't want the blood money, so they used it to buy a potter's field where tradition says Judas was buried."

"Judas would have made a great pirate, except for that hanging part."

"No, Henry, because traitors are the enemy of pirates and gentlemen alike. Gentlemen give their traitors a trial and then they hang them. We pirates maroon our traitors on sand bars at low tide with a pistol to kill themselves when the tide comes up."

"So, Jamison—the man they kept in the brig when they let Joshua and me out—is going to be tried in an Admiralty court and then be hung?"

"That's the way the civilized world does it, Henry."

"So, back to my question about why we're heading south if we're going to Savannah." He waited. "Are we going to hide the treasure in Kings Town?"

"Now, Henry, you know better than to ask me where I'm going to hide the treasure."

"What does that mean?"

"It means that you'll just have to wait to find out like everybody else."

☠ ☠ ☠

Two weeks later, the *Silver Cloud* and the *Remora* passed Tybee Island and sailed the fifteen miles up the Savannah River to Joshua Smoot's docks at Lamar's Creek where Willem and Sarah waited. Sarah and Willem watched as the lines were thrown across and the great ship was pulled to the dock.

"Something's wrong, Willem." She studied the several men standing at the rail. "I see Joshua and Henry, but I have never seen those that old man before, and none of those crewmen." She looked at the great ship's stern. "He left on *Le Tiburon* and he returns on the *Silver Cloud*."

"Something has happened, but since both Joshua and Henry are aboard, we must assume that it was nothing bad."

A few minutes later, the three stepped onto the dock and approached Sarah and Willem."

"Ha!" John Silver offered his hand. "You must be Willem Kesteren, the man who built this windmill and the rest of this."

"And who might you be, good sir?"

"I'm—"

"Why, this is the famous Long John Silver! He used to sail with John Flint."

"A lot has happened since you left!" He watched as the gangplank was pushed out and lowered to the dock. "I have hired Sarah as your accountant, and I can report that the mills and other businesses are running at capacity!"

"The Long John Silver? The pirate that parents threaten their children with?"

"That's me, wooden leg and all." He released Willem's hand and looked to the waterway. "This is where John Flint docked the *Walrus*, and now you've turned it into a thriving center of industry." He took Willem's hand. "I'm pleased to meet you Willem." He turned to Joshua. "Joshua told me about what you have done here. I am very impressed."

"What happened, Joshua?" Sarah pointed up at the ship. "You left aboard *Le Tiburon*, and you return on this frigate with that Virginia sharp in your wake."

"Oh, that." Silver gave her an apologetic shrug. "Nothing has gone well for your brother this past month. Sarah."

"Oh?"

"It's a long story that's best told over a glass of spirits." He gave her a wink. "Joshua tells me that High Tortuga is well stocked."

"It is but…" Sarah took Joshua's hand. "I need to take Joshua up to the mansion to show him something important." She gave an apologetic nod. "Do any of you mind?"

"I was hoping to show him what we've accomplished since he's been gone." Willem spread his arms. "But this will still be here tomorrow."

"My brother and I have some catching up to do." She led him to her carriage and called back. "We'll be up at High Tortuga waiting for you!"

Ten minutes later, Joshua and Sarah entered the mansion's foyer and walked across to Joshua's study. He stepped to the sideboard, took a glass, and filled it with rum.

"What happened at Dead Man's Chest, and where is *Le Tiburon*?"

"That's the treasure ship, and the treasure is in her lazarette." He emptied the glass. "That other ship is the *Remora*, and it belongs to John Silver."

"Then, if you have the treasure ship and the treasure, why would you say that everything that we planned went wrong?"

"We arrived at Christiansted two days before he *Eagle*, and took the crew without a fight. The *Silver Cloud* arrived right on schedule, anchored outside the reef, and the officers took most of the crew ashore to dig up the treasure."

"Go on."

"As I ordered, Nate Pritchard had already put thirty of his men ashore to attack them when they began digging, and at the same time, my spy released the *Silver Cloud*'s anchor to put them on the reef."

"Then what went wrong?"

"Robert Ormerod suspected we would be watching, so he led his men to a false location. Pritchard attacked, and both the *Silver Cloud* and *Le Tiburon* were damaged."

She pointed toward the windmill. "That *Silver Cloud*?"

"Yes, and we expected it to take them a week, but they finished their repairs the next day, dug up the treasure at dusk, and were back to sea before midnight."

"Where is *Le Tiburon*?"

"I ordered Pritchard to attack the *Silver Cloud*, and the battle went the wrong way." He gave a huff. "That night while the *Silver Cloud* was anchored near shore for repairs, they sent over several casks of rum laced with laudanum and took back the *Eagle*."

"So, who owns the treasure?"

"Long John Silver." He refilled his glass and took a sip. "Everything I just told you proves what I've always suspected, that your God hates me."

"You're wrong, Joshua. God loves you no matter what you have done—good or bad."

"Look at me. I'm a pirate, and the uneducated bastard son of John Flint. The only girl I have ever loved was forced to send me into slavery, and now she is gone. The governor of Georgia refused to grant me a letter of marque, and swears that if he catches me outside of Savannah, he'll send me to the gallows." He took a gulp of rum and coughed. "I've lost *Le Tiburon* and all the men who trusted me to make them rich." He stared at her for a long moment. "Where—in all that—do you see anything that tells you that God does not hate me?"

"If you'll listen to me for a few minutes, I will tell you why God doesn't hate you."

"How long is this going to take?"

"Will you—for just three or four minutes—pretend that there is a God?"

"If I must, to get that bottle from you."

"Being the businessman that you are, can you tell me how we humans determine the value of a certain thing?"

"That's simple, and it has nothing to do with whether you believe there's a God or not."

"Then tell me the simplicity of it, Joshua."

"A thing's value depends solely on what somebody is willing to pay for it."

"So, that gold ring you're wearing—if you held it up for auction—"

"Don't play games with me, Sarah. Get to your point."

"Well, since we're assuming that there is a God, and assuming that we human beings are worth something to Him, can you tell me what He was willing to pay for us?"

"Wait." Joshua remembered a similar conversation with Rebecca when they were in her secret garden. "When I was still in England—when I was hiding at Rebecca's secret garden—she asked that same question."

"Oh?" Sarah gave him a smile. "Tell me about your conversation with her."

"She asked me if I ever wanted something that I knew I could never afford, and then she asked me how the price was set."

"What did you tell her?"

"I told her that the person who is selling it sets the price, but she corrected me—that in the end, it is the price somebody is willing to pay that sets the real worth or value of the thing."

"Rebecca was right. A thing is only worth what somebody is willing to pay for it."

"Then…" He looked down in his empty glass while he thought back. "Then she asked me what God paid for me—for all mankind."

"And what did you tell her?"

"I told her what the Bible teaches us—what the Apostles told us—that God came and sacrificed himself on that Roman cross to redeem us from the devil."

"And how much did he pay for us, Joshua?"

"God paid the ultimate price—his very life."

"What does that tell you about your worth to God?"

Joshua considered and smiled. "You're right, Sarah. I'm worth so much to God that He would rather die than to lose me."

"Does that tell you whether God loves you or hates you?"

"What about all the sins I've committed? Don't I have to suffer for those sins?"

"No, because that's why Jesus went willing to that Roman cross as the Lamb of God. He did it to take away the sin of the world, and that includes all your sins."

"Then…"

"Do you remember what mother compared the gospel to?"

"She said…" It took him a moment. "She told us that the gospel was like the marriage proposal made by a man to the woman he loves—that God is asking us to marry him."

"Do you understand what that means?"

"Not really." He gave her a question look. "Do you?"

"Everything that God has done from the creation to this moment has been to bring us to Himself. He loves us—every one of us. He longs for us—His fiancé—to accept His marriage proposal to become his bride, and finally we—those who believe and trust Him—to become His wife."

"You're saying that we are to be God's wife?"

"Well, actually the bride of Christ, and that's the reason He did what He did on the cross." She waited. "Do you see it, Joshua—what you told me a moment ago about how a thing is valued?"

"I…"

"God considers you so valuable to Him that He did exactly what you said a moment ago—everything necessary to redeem and purchase us—you Joshua—from your chains and slavery." Joshua didn't answer, so Sarah continued. "If our Creator God considers you that valuable, then how can you say that you are worthless?" She did not wait for his answer. "The real chains and slavery are your self-pity—how you have polished that lie you keep telling yourself until it now shines like the false idol you have made it."

It took Joshua several breaths to answer. "I want to be left alone."

"Very well." Sarah handed him the bottle, turned, and walked out into the foyer. She stopped and turned back. "God is there, Joshua, and He wants you in heaven with Him. Whether you believe in Him or not doesn't change that fact." As she put her hand on the front door handle, she remembered why she brought him up to his mansion. "Wait!"

He picked up the bottle of rum. "What?"

"I have to show you something that will change everything." She walked back into the study, opened the desk drawer, and pulled out a journal and a rolled parchment. "Do you remember our conversation about my mother's personal journal and your mother's last will and testament?"

"Yes?"

"When you and Henry left for Dead Man's Chest, I decided to tear loose that rug and clean up my mother's blood. When I pried it up, a loose board came up with it."

"Oh?"

"You were right, Joshua." She held up the two items. "Until that moment, I had no proof except Damon Hobson's claims about your birth mother." She handed him the parchment. "You need to read this, because like I said, it changes everything."

He untied the blue ribbon and pulled it open. "What is this?"

"It's your mother's last will and testament in her own hand, and witnessed by my mother. It, along with my mother's personal journal, was hidden for all these years under my mother's blood."

Joshua read the document silently.

This, the Last Will and Testament of Elaine MacBride, 4ᵗʰ Marchioness of Earlshall:

I write this, my Last Will and Testament, in shame. For the last eight months in which I have been living as the unwilling Concubine of Pirate Captain John Flint at the home of the Midwife, Emily Smoot. David MacBride and I were married at the home of my Mother, Jane Frederick, on the 2ⁿᵈ day of June 1747 at Edinburgh, Scotland, me being pregnant one month. To avoid the embarrassment to which we would be exposed, David and I booked passage to America where we would honeymoon and spend our first year of marriage away from Scotland. We traveled from Earlshall Castle to Edinburgh where we boarded the merchant ship Fortune. After five weeks at sea, our ship was attacked by Pirates in a ship named Walrus under the command of John Flint. The men who were not killed outright were set at sea in the ship's boats. That was the last I saw of my husband, David MacBride. I was taken in the Walrus to Savannah, Georgia where John Flint kept me in slavery. When he went to sea, I was handed over to Constable Damon Hobson who forced me to live with the Midwife, Emily Smoot—threatening to accuse me of witchcraft and prostitution if I left that place. John Flint would go to sea for several weeks, and when he returned, Damon Hobson took me to the Pirate. Today is the 29ᵗʰ day of January 1748. I have given birth to a son, to whom I leave all my earthly belongings. He has a birthmark at the base of his spine in the shape of a shark (picture). I am dying from the bleeding that Emily Smoot cannot stop. I have asked her to tell John Flint that it was a girl and that she died with me. May the Lord have mercy on my soul.

Given under my hand this 29ᵗʰ day of January 1748.

Elaine MacBride

Marchioness of Earlshall

Witness: Emily Smoot, Midwife

Joshua looked up at her. "Her signature."

"What?"

"I need to show you something I got from Damon Hobson." He was gone for several minutes and returned with the bundle of letters. "Look at these."

"Letters?"

"They are eight letters that Damon Hobson claimed my mother sent to her mother in Edinburgh." He pointed at the signature on the will. "Until now, I had no way of verifying that they were truly written by my mother's hand." He set them next to the will and opened the top letter. "Look. The signatures are identical."

"If she sent them to Edinburgh, how did Damon get them?"

"He had a spy in the postal house who set them aside for him."

Sarah reached across and touched them. "I assume you've read all eight."

"Of course, I have." Joshua held up the first letter. "This is the only one where she described the abduction and how John Flint brought her here to Savannah and boarded with your mother. The rest of it is her begging that somebody be sent to rescue and to find David." He picked up the other seven letters. "The rest of her letters were pleading for rescue."

"And they never got to her mother."

"The last letter made me cry, Sarah, because it was clear that she had given up and resigned herself to her captivity."

Just then, there was laughter as Silver, Kesteren, Archer, and Morgan came through the front door and called from the foyer. "Sarah! Joshua! We're here, and we need a draft of those spirits you promised us!"

Joshua called back. "We're in here—in the study!"

"Ah!" Silver stepped to the door and spotted the bottle of rum. "Everybody! Get a glass so we can raise them in a toast to our recent success!"

"Wait, John." Joshua held up the parchment. "You need to read this first."

"What is it?"

"Remember when we were talking about the crest on my ring and how you had done some research into my possible past?"

"Aye?"

He touched the journal. "This is Emily Smoot's personal journal that chronicles the eight months my mother lived with her before I was born." He held out the parchment. "This is my mother's last will and testament in her own hand. I've compared it to the eight letters she tried to send to her mother in Edinburgh, and they are a match."

"Really!"

"It's the proof we needed that the crest on this ring has been trying to tell me all these years." He handed John Silver the will. "Read this to everybody."

When John Silver was finished, he looked at Joshua. "This changes everything."

"Yes, it does." Silver turned and looked at the others.

He held up the parchment. "But now that I've read your mother's testament, there are important things I must do."

"What kind of things?"

"I need to sail north to Charles Town to speak with Joseph Reed—the young man you know as Tommy Clark."

"The lad I let help sail *Amazing Grace* to Kings Town?"

"General Washington sent him to shepherd the cannons. He has been with them every minute, all the way from Falkirk over a year ago to when they finally reached Charles Town a few days ago."

"What business do you have with him, and how does my mother's testament change things?"

"A lot depends on what the general has to say, so I can't tell you right now." He gave the young pirate a smile. "You'll just have to trust me."

"What about the treasure?"

"For now, it's safest in the *Silver Cloud*'s lazarette."

Then…" Joshua looked east toward the docks. "Are you trusting Morgan and me to watch over it for you?"

"Yes, you two and the rest of these fine people who work for you."

"When are you leaving?"

"Tomorrow morning, and I should only be gone a week." Silver turned to Sarah. "I'll need to take your mother's will, her journal, and one of her letters with me."

"Of course." She handed him the journal.

Joshua handed him the letters. "Why would General Washington need to read these?"

"Trust me, Joshua."

"Wait."

"For what?"

"Before you do whatever it is that I must trust you for, I have question to ask you that you may find difficult to answer."

"How difficult?"

"Were you on the *Walrus* when Flint took my mother captive and killed my father?"

"I was, but it didn't mean anything to me."

"What? How could you watch such a terrible thing and not care?"

"Oh, I cared, but since Flint did the same thing every time, he took a prize, it was not something that I could do anything about."

"Did you see him kill my father?"

"No." Silver gave a raise of his shoulders. "The men who put up a fight were killed outright, but the others—the ones who cooperated—were put adrift in the ship's boats."

"What about the women?"

"Flint gave the plain women to the crew, but he always took the prettiest one for himself."

"What about me? Were you part of the *Walrus* crew when I was kidnapped to England?"

"I well remember that trip to Brighton, and I well remember that there was a lad named Tommy chained to the main mast for a week or so at the beginning of the trip."

"I don't remember seeing you."

"John Flint threatened that if any of us was caught being kind to you that we would be flogged. That's why I kept my distance."

"So, you ignored me?"

Not completely, Joshua. There was a moment—"

"When!"

"The day Jasper was flogged and then thrown to the sharks. When your chain was pulling you across the deck to your doom, I stepped on it with my left foot just before Flint pinioned your hand to the deck with that pike pole."

"Then you did care."

"You were none of my business, but it seemed a waste to see you drown."

☠ ☠ ☠

Later that evening John Silver took up a quill and dipped it in the ink well.

My dearest Lady Frederick,

My name is Long John Silver. I was part of John Flint's crew when your granddaughter and her husband were attacked on their way to America over twenty-five years ago. While David MacBride was set adrift with several others who survived the attack, John Flint took Elaine to Savannah as his mistress, and kept her at the home of the Midwife, Emily Smoot. Elaine was pregnant by her husband, David MacBride. When her pregnancy began to show, Flint lost interest in her, but believed that she carried his child. The Savannah constable—an evil man named Damon Hobson—waited until Elaine's baby was born. When he discovered that the baby was a boy, and that Elaine had died shortly thereafter from uncontrollable bleeding, Hobson lied to John Flint that his bastard was a stillborn daughter. When the lad reached eight years old, Hobson went to Flint and demanded thirty pieces of silver to take him to his bastard son. When Flint took Joshua away, he killed Emily Smoot, and her blood dripped down through the floorboards.

Emily's ten-year-old daughter Sarah covered the pool of blood with a throw rug and only recently tore it up. As she did, a loose board remained attached to the rug, revealing Emily's secret stash. In it, Sarah found her mother's life savings, her personal journal, and Elaine MacBride's Last Will and Testament. I have copied the complete document in my hand and enclose it with this letter. I will sail to Edinburgh in six weeks. My ship is the Remora, a Virginia Sharp Schooner with dark red sails. This letter will precede me by several weeks, so if you will leave word for me at the Court of the Lord Lyon, I will bring the documents and your grandson, Joshua Smoot, to you at your home.

By my hand this 10ᵗʰ day of July 1775,

Long John Silver

CHAPTER SIXTEEN:
Silver meets Washington

*A*s John Silver made ready to depart for Charles Town, Willem arrived by carriage and called from the dock. "On the *Remora*! Is John Silver aboard!"

Silver climbed from the hold and walked across to the rail. "I'm here, Willem!"

Willem walked up the gangway and looked at the rigging and across the deck. "Is there anything on the *Remora* that needs repair before you depart?"

"There is one thing." Silver pointed at the *Silver Cloud*. "As you know, Joshua and Henry still want the treasure."

"I know, and between Sarah and me, they will be kept away from the ship and everything on it."

"Thank you."

"How long will I need to police them?

"If everything goes as I expect, within a week."

"John!" It was Daniel Archer. "We're ready to sail! Shall I give the order?"

"Aye! Give the order!"

Willem returned to the dock and called. "May you have fair seas and following winds, Captain Silver!"

"Thank you!"

The trip from Savannah to the Forrestal shipyard at Charles Town took a day and a half. The *Remora* eased to the dock just as the sun was setting. As expected, Joseph Reed was waiting as the lines were thrown across and the gangway was lowered to the dock.

"Welcome to Charles Town, Mister Silver!"

"Thank you, Joseph!" Silver carried his bag down to the dock and took the offered hand. "Is the general here?"

"No, but he has been sent for. I expect that he should be here early tomorrow morning."

"Have you and he spoken about the treasure ship—my *Silver Cloud*?"

"Yes, but without knowing what you have in mind, we can only speculate at this time."

"And what might your speculations be?"

"Well, obviously that you want us to buy the ship back from you."

"Interesting." Silver looked toward the buildings. "I'm hungry, my back hurts, and I need a bath."

"Ha! I can arrange to have those needs satisfied." He pointed to his carriage. "Shall we?"

Alex Forrestal was waiting at the front portico of his mansion when the two arrived.

"Alex Forrestal, this is Captain John Silver, the present owner of the *Silver Cloud* that carried the treasure back from Dead Man's Chest."

"Uh…" He refused to take the offered hand. "I beg to differ with my young friend, Mister Silver. The *Silver Cloud* that you took to Kings Town belongs to me."

"Well, I beg to differ with you, Mister Forrestal, and I will be negotiating with General Washington about her return, not with you."

"But I built her. I put up most of the money for her construction."

"I understand, but she is in my possession, not yours."

"We'll see about that when the general gets here in the morning."

"Please, Alex." Joseph stepped between the two. "I've promised Captain Silver a hot bath, a warm meal, and a soft bed. After dinner, we can share several glasses of rum. Perhaps the spirits from the bottle will calm the angry spirit you carry in your heart."

The next morning, just as breakfast was being served, General Washington entered Alex Forrestal's home, took a deep breath, and called out. "Have I missed Breakfast?"

"Is that you, General?" Alex pushed back his chair and walked out to the entry hall. "We sat down five minutes ago, and there is enough for a half dozen more just like you."

"Wonderful!" He swept his hand toward the dining room. "Lead the way, my good friend."

"Uh…" Alex put a hand to the general's arm and lowered his voice. "Before we sit down with Captain Silver, a word concerning the other *Silver Cloud*."

"Have you and Captain Silver already begun haggling over a price?"

"No, it's the same problem I've been harping on since the cannons arrived."

"I understand your concern, my old friend." George gave Alex a comforting smile. "You claim that since you built both ships, they both belong to you."

"Of course, they do."

"But Long John Silver and his people are in possession of her, and even if you are right, if we try to take her by force, they could run her out to sea and scuttle her before we could stop them."

"So, you're willing to pay that pirate good money—money we need to finance this war with England—for the return of what already belongs to us?"

"Please, Alex." He took a step toward the dining room. "Let's see what the man has to say before we start making threats."

"I haven't threatened Captain Silver. I just—"

"I'm starving, Alex, and the smell of fried bacon is making my stomach churn."

"Very well." Alex led the way and returned to his chair. "General Washington, this is Captain John Silver."

"Pleased to meet you, sir." Silver shook the general's hand and sat back down. "How was your trip down from Boston?"

"Long and tiring." He filled his plate with eggs, bacon, and potatoes. "How was your sail up from Savannah?"

"Fairly uneventful, considering."

"Considering what?"

"Well, we came upon a coaster that was low in the water, which, if you know much about sailing ships, meant that she was carrying a heavy load." He gave a smile. "My crew insisted that we fire a shot across her bow, board her, and take a look at her cargo."

"Are you serious?" Alex threw down his fork and stood. "After all that we've done to set up this meeting with the general, you'd jeopardize it by an act of piracy?"

"Ha!" Silver stuck a full slice of bacon into his mouth and chewed it slowly. "I'm just kidding with you, Alex. There was no coaster, and the only things aboard the *Remora* are my crew and the provisions we needed for this trip."

"Please, gentlemen." George set down his fork and wiped the egg from his mouth. "Can we put our personal feelings aside long enough to finish breakfast without one of you challenging the other to a duel?"

"I'm sorry General." Alex sat back down. "But he's a pirate, and you heard—"

"Calm down, Alex. It was only a joke."

"I'll calm down, but he has to stop antagonizing me."

When breakfast was finished and the plates were taken away, General Washington looked to John Silver. "You called for this meeting, Captain Silver, so please state your business."

"Yes, I am the famous blood-thirsty pirate that parents use to make their children behave." He gave Alex a quick glance and raise of his bushy brows. "But I am also a man who knows a lot about what is going on between America and England."

"Such as?"

"I know that your army is ill-equipped, under-trained, and under paid."

"I neither agree or deny your assertion, Captain Silver."

"I also know that much of this coming war against England will be fought at sea where the tools of war are transported." He paused. "The Continental Navy is not yet born, yet you need a navy right now to stop the importation of arms and ammunition to the British forces that have established themselves in and around Boston."

"How do you know this?"

Silver turned to Alex. "The prosperous pirates pay for spies to keep track of everything that happens in the colonies and at sea. I have a dozen such men who owe me debts they can never repay." He turned back to the general. "You, General Washington, have it within your power to create your own navy."

"And how am I to do that?"

"You need to create a fleet of armed privateers." Silver held up a finger. "As certain as night follows day, without a dedicated and decisive naval force, we can do nothing to counter the abuses of the King. With that effective naval force, we can do everything honorable and glorious."

The general sat back and pursed his lips. "Many of my officers have nautical experience and abilities, and there must be dozens of seaworthy vessels that could carry cannons."

"You know that piracy and privateering are the same, except for one important thing."

"Yes—a letter of marque." The general considered for a moment. "Then what I need to do is recruit privateer captains from wherever I can find them, provide them with patriotic volunteers who are eager to turn their special skills against their former country."

"Which brings me to the matter of the *Silver Cloud* that is presently tied up at a dock at Savannah."

"I don't want to hear this." Alex stood and pushed back his chair. "That ship has already cost me—"

"Enough, Alex!" The general pointed at the man. "Sit down!" He turned to Silver. "We're listening, Captain Silver."

"Granted, pirates have followed a dark career that has earned them the gallows. But most of us were forced into the brotherhood—as we call it—by circumstances such as poverty, by kidnapping, or one of a score of other reasons. Our strategy is to become wealthy so that we can enjoy the pleasures that the gifted and otherwise elite in society take for granted. The tactics we use to achieve that goal are often cruel and bloody."

"Where is this going, Captain Silver/"

"Joshua Smoot was tricked by two evil men—the result being that his betrothed was forced to either have him sold into slavery or hung from a yardarm while she was forced to watch. That cruel act by a man who wanted his fiancé for himself, drove Joshua into slavery and eventually piracy."

"Get to your point, John."

"Joshua doesn't know that I am advocating like this on his behalf, so if you agree to my proposal, you will have to promise me that you will allow me to disclose the thing to him when and where I choose."

"That's easy enough. What is it that you want me to grant to Joshua Smoot?"

"To create your navy of privateers, you will be creating dozens of letters of marque. I am willing to hand over to you and Mister Forrestal my *Silver Cloud* in exchange for two letters of marque—one for me and one for Joshua Smoot."

"No!" Alex raised his hands in protest. "He's a pirate—known from Boston to Jamaica! If you do that, you will bring disgrace upon everything that we—"

"Alex is right. If I issue him such a letter, he will have to accept it in another name."

"I…" Silver pinched his lip in thought. "John Manley! When I sent him to New York in a failed attempt to get Robert Ormerod to provide me a map of Dead Man's Chest, he used that name."

"I agree to your terms." He looked at Joseph and got a nod. He turned to Alex. "Are you happy, my old friend?"

"Yes, but I don't understand why he would do that—trade a ship worth twenty-thousand dollars for a piece of paper."

Silver turned to Alex. "Pirates are like all other men. We want a legacy." He turned to the general. "When you write your history books, tell your grandchildren about Long John Silver, how he and Joshua—John Manley—helped free America from the cruel tentacles of England and King James."

"Yes. I will make sure that our history books mention what you and he have done for America."

"And what are you going to tell them—the people in Savannah—that you are getting in exchange for handing over the *Silver Cloud*?"

"He's right." The old pirate turned to the ship builder. "What do you suggest I tell them?"

A silence fell over the four men for several moments.

"Sir." Joseph turned to the general. "Is there a way to cancel the King's warrants for these men—Silver, Smoot, Morgan—and for the men who crewed their ships?"

"I…"

"A congressional pardon?"

"We are still under the Crown, Joseph. The King's warrants cannot be cancelled with a pardon from a revolutionary continental general."

"The question that Alex and Mister Silver posed has to do with how he will explain his return of the *Silver Cloud* without a payment."

"What if he tells them that there will be a payment, and that it will be delivered after the *Silver Cloud* is safely back here at my ship_yard?"

"That would be a lie, Alex." The general looked at Silver. "Would they be satisfied with a letter from me giving them immunity—that they will not be pursued by any American entities—and that we will not turn them over to the Crown for prosecution?"

"Yes." Silver gave the general a nod. "I can convince them that they are the victors with a letter from you with those promises."

"I will write the letter, Mister Silver."

"Then we have our agreement." He turned to Alex. "I will return to Savannah and arrange for the release of the *Silver Cloud*."

That afternoon, with the two letters from General Washington in hand, Long John Silver posted his letter to Jane Frederick and departed Charles Town for Savannah.

CHAPTER SEVENTEEN:
Remora to Edinburgh

*A*s expected, the *Remora* was met at the Savannah docks by Joshua, Elizabeth, Willem, Henry, and Sarah.

"Well?" Joshua called out to Silver while the last line was secured and the gangway was being lowered. "What are they paying us for the *Silver Cloud*?"

"This!" Silver held up the letter from General Washington.

"What is that?"

"It's better than money, Joshua." Silver walked down the gangway.

"You're giving them the *Silver Cloud* for a letter?"

"No." He handed the letter to the young pirate. "General Washington has given us our freedom."

"Freedom from what?"

"Freedom from the gallows."

"He can do that?" Sarah and Willem looked over Joshua's shoulders as he read the pardon. Joshua looked up. "But we are already protected by the merchants and our monthly payments to the constable and his men."

"That protection is only good here in Savannah, but what the merchants have promised us has no teeth once we leave Savannah." Joshua opened his mouth to protest but Silver continued. "General Washington told me that if he wanted, he could send a contingent of armed soldiers here to arrest us and take the *Silver Cloud* from us by force."

Joshua looked up from the letter. "He says that he'll also protect us from the King. Can he do that?"

"You read his words. He will in no way assist the Crown to find or arrest any of us." Silver pointed at the document. "That is as good as a pardon from King James himself."

Henry stepped forward. "What now, Captain Silver?"

"Now, it is time for us to sail to Scotland where we will prove that Joshua is the titled son of David and Elaine MacBride."

Sarah looked up from the document. "You've already written to the Court of the Lord Lyon?"

"I posted a letter several days ago to Elaine's mother, Lady Jane Frederick. I told her that Elizabeth, Joshua, and I will be arriving in six weeks at Edinburgh."

Joshua pointed at the *Silver Cloud*. "What about the treasure?"

"When we're ready to leave, we will divide it—leaving a third of it here to be added to the business." He looked to Willem and Sarah. "You two will be in charge of it while we are gone."

So…" Henry looked at Willem and Sarah, and back to Silver. "What about the five shares Joshua promised me? Will I get that when we reach Scotland?"

"You'll get your five shares from what we are leaving here."

"You're not taking me with you?"

"You have the mind of a pirate, Henry. You would only be in the way in Scotland."

"Then…what am I supposed to do here?"

"That's up to you." Silver pointed to the general's letter. "You can learn to run one of these businesses under Willem and Sarah and be a free man, or you can go back to sea as a pirate and take your chances with the King's gallows."

Willem put a hand on the lad's shoulder. "Don't worry, Henry. Sarah and I will find a job for you and teach you everything you need to know."

☠ ☠ ☠

Six weeks later, the *Remora* crept forward along the Newhaven Harbor docks under reefed sails searching for an open space to tie up. As they approached the west end, a small lad ran ahead of a black lacquered carriage shouting and pointed at the approaching ship.

"It's them! I told you they were here!" The boy stopped at an opening and waved his arms. "Here! You can tie up here!"

While the *Remora* crept to the dock, one of the crew threw his line across to the boy. Within minutes, the gangway was in place, allowing John and Elizabeth to step down to the dock.

The boy ran to the carriage and jumped up on the step. "It's them, Miss Jane! They're here!"

The footman helped the woman down to the worn planks. "Well, well! The famous Long John Silver!" The tall woman turned to Elizabeth. "And this must be your beautiful wife, Elizabeth." Jane gave Elizabeth a warm embrace.

The boy tapped Jane on the arm. "Is that really him?"

"Yes—that's Long John Silver."

"Sir?" The boy looked up at the old pirate and spoke the words slowly. "Do you really eat children's hearts?"

"Oh, no!" Silver gave a laugh and a shake of his head. " John Flint eats children's hearts, but he died many years ago—long before you were born."

Jane gave a laugh. "When our children misbehave, we threaten them with stories like that." Jane pulled a note from her sleeve and handed it to the boy. "Roger. Take this to the man I told you about, and wait there for his answer."

Silver looked to the carriage. "We didn't expect such a grand reception."

"You told me in your letter that the *Remora* is a Virginia s harp schooner with dark red sails, so I hired Roger to watch for your arrival." She looked to the deck where Joshua stood. "Is that him? Is that my grandson?"

"Aye." He turned as Joshua made his way down the gangway and stepped to the woman. "Joshua. It gives me great pleasure to introduce you to your grandmother, Lady Jane Frederick."

"Can we begin with a hug?" She stepped to him with outstretched arms. "With a grandmother embracing her grandson for the first time?"

"Yes, Ma'am."

"Call me Grandma." Jane took Joshua into her arms and rained kisses on his cheeks. She pulled back and inspected his face. "Except for that scar on your cheek-, you are the image of your father, with a sprinkling of your mother through your eyes and your mouth."

"I never knew either of them."

"I know. That was a terrible thing John Flint did to David and Elaine." She reached up and touched the scar. "And then the things he did to you…"

"But I survived, Ma'am—Grandma—and look at where I am now." He spread his arms. "I might have a Scottish title."

Silver cleared his throat. "That's why we're here—to establish that very thing." He took Elizabeth's hand. "I don't want to cut this reunion short, but I'm anxious to know what you've found."

"I have already spoken with my good friend, John Hooke-Campbell, and he's already read the letter you sent me."

"Who is that?"

"Why, he's none other than the Lord Lyon King of Arms—the man who has the final judgement whether Joshua is who Elaine says he is." She pointed to her carriage. "Let's the four of us take this conversation to my home."

Ten minutes later, Jane escorted Elizabeth and the two men into her two-story home. "Mister Atwood will take your bags up to your rooms." She walked to the sitting room, stepped to the desk, and opened the drawer.

"These are the two letters Elaine sent me just before she and David departed for America." She handed them to John. "As you can see, she signed them as Elaine MacBride."

John reached into his pocket and pulled out the eight letters. "Then you'll want these."

"What are they?"

"Your daughter wrote these letters to you begging that you rescue her, but the man who held her prisoner didn't allow them to leave Savannah."

"When word came to me that the Fortune had been taken by pirates, I hoped that Elaine's life was spared, but when I never received a letter from her, it confirmed my worst fears." She put the letters to her lips for several moments and then looked at John. "Thank you for bringing me these."

He handed her the will. "This is her last will and testament—the original."

"Oh, my Lord." She looked up at him. "Is this my daughter's blood?"

"No. It's Emily Smoot's blood—the woman who raised Joshua and gave him her name."

She untied the ribbon, spread the parchment on the desk and set weights on the four corners. Tears welled in her eyes as she read her daughter's final words. She looked up at Joshua. "I did this to her."

"What?"

"She came to me." Jane wiped the tears away. "When she told me that she was pregnant with you, I was the one who arranged their rushed marriage, and I was the one who told them to sail away to America to avoid the scandal."

"But you couldn't know that the pirates—that John Flint would do what he did."

"But don't you see, Joshua?" She struck herself on the chest. "I was more worried about what people would think of me than for the danger that might happen to Elaine and David." She took several labored breaths. "I killed my daughter and her husband. I sold you into those chains and slavery that ultimately forced you into piracy."

Joshua put a comforting arm around her shoulders. "Both good and bad things happen to each one of us, but we must remember that God is watching over us." He looked down at the letters Jane set next to the parchment. "Will these documents be enough proof?"

"It should be, and this drawing of Joshua's birthmark will connect him to the will." She looked at Joshua. "Do you mind?"

"We've sailed several thousand miles to prove her will is speaking of me." He took off his coat, unfastened his belt, and turned his back to her.

"Pardon my cold hands, Joshua. I'm nervous." She pushed the waist band down in the back two inches. "There it is—exactly like her drawing."

"There is more." Joshua pulled up his trousers and held out his left hand to her. "The ring. Sarah Smoot—my sister—gave this to me. She told me that my father gave it to my mother as a wedding gift."

"Sarah was correct." She studied the crest. "I was there when he gave it to her."

"So, will this help also when we meet with Mister Campbell?"

"Oh, yes. Most assuredly."

"Do we have an appointment with him?"

"Not yet. Not until Roger—the boy that asked you about eating hearts— returns with the answer to my inquiry." She looked at the clock and gave the two a smile. "You must be hungry."

"Aye!" Silver gave a laugh. "We're hungry and we need a bath with soap and fresh water."

"Mister Atwood is preparing your three baths as we speak." She looked at the clock. "Dinner will be at five o'clock."

When the three returned to the parlor an hour later, Jane was holding a note. "Roger brought back the answer. We have an appointment with Mister Campbell at ten tomorrow morning."

"Wonderful!" Silver ran his hands down his fresh clothes. "Betty and I had almost forgotten how good a hot bath could revive a person's soul."

Jane turned to Joshua. "Naturally, you know that I have dozens of questions."

"Oh, yes." Joshua gave a nod. "Where do you want me to start?"

"At the beginning—in Savannah. What are your first memories?"

"Age two, I believe. I had everything a lad could want. A loving mother and sister who provided all my needs and taught me to read, write, and do my sums." He gave her a smile. "I even took care of a cat that showed up on our doorstep."

Atwood stepped to the doorway. "Dinner is served, Ma'am."

"Thank you, Atwood." She turned to her three guests. "I hope you like lamb."

"It's our favorite." Elizabeth stood and reached for her husband's hand. "Shall we?"

Once seated, Jane put her hands in her lap, closed her eyes, and prayed. "Dear Lord, we thank you for this wonderful day and the safe arrival of these three special people. We thank you for this meal, and we look forward to your soon return. In Jesus' name, Amen."

With each course, Joshua recounted a separate period in his life.

"So, you were sold into slavery for protecting your fiancé from that captain's son?"

"Yes, and they forced Rebecca to decide whether I would be sent into slavery or executed."

"Did those two—Captain Drake and his son—every pay for their crime against you and Rebecca?"

"Yes." He held up his hand. "They both died at this hand."

Jane sat back and wiped her mouth with her linen. "Shall we take our wine to the parlor and talk about the future?"

"That would be good." Silver took his goblet and the wine bottle. "The future is the place where we store our dreams."

"Oh, my." She gave John a tilt of her head. "A famous pirate and a poet.?"

"No, simply a man of many dreams and desires."

"What about you, Joshua? What are your dreams and desires?"

"Piracy is a dangerous profession. For that reason, my desire—my dream— has been to acquire a letter of marque from one of the American governors so that I can continue the life I love but without the threat of the British gallows."

"And what about you two? You and Elizabeth are my age. What are you desiring?"

"We have the same desire." He reached across and took Elizabeth's hand. "Betty and I are tired of striving to survive, so once Joshua's matter is settled, we plan to return to either Kings Town or Savannah to live out our lives in ease."

"Well, if tomorrow goes as I expect it to, your desire may become a reality here in Scotland."

"You talk as though you already know what the Lord Lyon will determine even before he's seen our evidence."

"Mister Campbell and I grew up together, and the moment I received your letter, I took it to him. He told me that he needed three things—to read her last will and testament, to confirm her handwriting, and to see Joshua's birth mark."

"This may be presumptuous of me, Jane, but if Mister Campbell grants Joshua a title, what will that mean?"

"It means that Joshua will become the Marquess of Earlshall, and the Lord of the Earlshall Castle—a 53-acre estate on the northern edge of Saint Andrews Bay." She pointed north. "It's about thirty miles up the coast."

☠ ☠ ☠

The next morning, the four walked up the steps of the stone two-story building and were met by a representative of the court.

"Good morning, Jamie. Is Mister Campbell ready to receive us?"

"Yes." He looked at the old pirate. "Is that him—Long John Silver?"

Silver gave a laugh. "How is it that the Scots know so much about me?"

"You're a legend—you and John Flint." He looked at Joshua. "And if what I've heard from the Lord Lyon about Joshua Smoot is true, he will become a legendary pirate also." Jamie pointed down the hallway. "Shall we?"

"Ah!" The Lord Lyon stood and gave Jane an embrace. "Sharon sends her appreciation for the shawl you crocheted for her birthday."

"I received her letter yesterday."

"And these two gentlemen." He turned and offered his hand to Silver. "You must be the famous Long John Silver that Jane has told me was coming to Edinburgh."

"I am pleased to meet you, Mister Campbell." He turned to Joshua. "This is Jane's grandson, Joshua Smoot."

"Joshua Smoot?" He looked to Jane. "If he's the son of David and Elaine MacBride, as Jane has assured me that he is, shouldn't his surname be MacBride?"

"Yes but…" She looked to Joshua. "Maybe you can explain it quicker than me."

"I was born on 29 January 1748 at the home of the Savannah midwife, Emily Smoot. She kept my identity a secret from John Flint until the local constable, Damon Hobson, figured I was old enough to apprentice as a pirate on Flint's ship, the *Walrus*." He gave Silver a quick glance and continued. "While my sister Sarah and were forced to watch, John Flint shot our mother—my adopted mother—and then he kidnapped me to England. When I refused to take the name of Thomas Flint, I was treated like a slave." He stopped and took several breaths. "That is why I have gone by the name, Joshua Smoot all these years."

"Did you know any of this, Mister Silver?"

"Regrettably, I was part of John Flint's crew when he set David MacBride adrift and took Elaine as his concubine." He looked to Jane. "As I explained to Jane and Joshua, Flint did that every time there were women on the ships we took as prizes. The plain women were handed over to the crew while he took the fairest for himself." Silver gave a huff. "It was such a common occurrence that none of us objected."

"Oh, my." Campbell looked to Jane. "We live here in Edinburgh in such a protected world."

"I am realizing that more and more." She opened her satchel and pulled out the parchment and the letters. "Here are the documents."

"Yes." It took the Lord Lyon only minutes to make his judgement. "There is no doubt that you are in fact the son of David and Elaine MacBride, and the new owner of the Earlshall Castle."

She gave Silver a nudge and whispered. "I told you, didn't I?"

"Yes." Silver turned to Campbell. "Jane told us about the place, but I have a question."

"I would imagine you and Joshua have many questions."

"Who lives there now, and where will they go when we move in?"

"Only the staff and grounds keepers." He gave a knowing nod. "I know it's been many years that David and Elaine MacBride have been absent from the place, but this is how it is done in Scotland."

"Then..?"

"Jane told me that you came here in your own ship. You can sail to the castle's docks on the north coast of Saint Andrews Bay. The castle is less than a mile from there, and I have informed the staff of your soon arrival."

Jane turned to the three. "But before you take my grandson away, could you and Elizabeth stay here in Edinburgh for a few more days so we can catch up on the years that we've lost?"

"Betty and I are here as your most grateful guests." He gave a nod. "Of course, we'll stay, and as long as you want."

CHAPTER EIGHTEEN:

Joshua's Letter of Marque

Twenty minutes later, the four stepped into Jane's home. They were met by Atwood, the butler. "Welcome home, Lady Frederick. From your smile, I must assume everything went as you hoped."

"Yes, exactly as I knew it would." She gave him a touch to his arm. "We would like tea in the parlor"

"Yes, Ma'am."

Once settled, Jane turned to Joshua. "Tell me about your childhood in Savannah. Were you a happy boy?"

"Very happy. I have a sister who is two years older than me that acted as my nanny. We had toys to play with. There was a garden behind our home that I helped tend. Women came to our home to have their babies." He paused. "I was a happy boy until the day John Flint took me away to England."

"That had to be awful—you and all those pirates—and nobody on your side."

"Ben Gunn tried to be my friend, and even offered to take my punishment once." He gave Silver an accusing look. "There were some who ignored me, but there were others who would risk a flogging by bringing me food."

"Why did he bring you to England?"

"To change my name to Thomas Flint, and have me educated and raised as a gentleman."

"What happened? Why did you turn to piracy?"

"Jane." It was Elizabeth. "It's a long and bitter story that covered several years." She gave a grimace. "Better for another time."

"Of course." She turned to Joshua. "If you don't want to talk about it, I understand."

☠ ☠ ☠

On the fourth morning, John, Elizabeth, and Joshua set sail for Saint Andrew's Bay. It was a short trip—taking only four hours. They were met by a man and a woman—the butler and housekeeper of the castle.

Clive received the lines that the crew threw across. "Welcome to the Earlshall estate! My name is Clive Shepherd, and this is my wife, Mary!"

Mary looked at the three. "You have to be Long John Silver, and you must be his faithful wife, Elizabeth." She turned to Joshua. "And you! You are the new Lord of Earlshall Castle."

"That's what the Lord Lyon at Arms has told us."

"What shall we call you?"

"Well, for nearly thirty years I've been known as Joshua Smoot."

"Then you should be Marquess Joshua MacBride."

With the last line secured and the gangway lowered, the three walked down to the dock. Silver turned back to Captain Archer. "Once the ship is secured, we'll send the carriage back for you ."

The carriage ride was short—a little less than a mile. After introducing the three to the staff and showing them their rooms, Clive suggested a grand tour of the castle and the grounds.

"That would be wonderful." Mary turned to Elizabeth. "That will give us a chance to get to know each other." As they walked through the main hall, Mary and Elizabeth fell behind. "How often does Lady Jane come to the castle?"

"She spends most of her time at her home in Edinburgh, but now that Joshua is here, I would expect to see much more of her."

"This is incredible." Elizabeth touched one of the tapestries. "Who pays for all this—to keep it so clean and running so well?"

"The estate is self-sufficient. We raise a special breed of sheep, and their wool is highly prized around the world." Mary stopped in the parlor as the men walked away toward the armory. "You have to understand something about Lady Jane. She is a woman of great faith, and once she knew about her daughter's pregnancy, she has always believed that the Lord would bring Elaine and her grandchild home."

"So, you've known all this time that Elaine was with child before she and David were married?"

"I heard crying that day, so I went to make sure Lady Jane was alright. As I stepped near her bedroom door, I heard Elaine blurt it out to her mother." She gave Elizabeth a pained look. "I retreated and never let either of them know that I knew their secret."

"So, you and Clive, and the rest of the staff has been waiting all these years for Joshua's arrival?"

"Yes, but we didn't know if the child would be a boy or a girl, or whether there would even be such a reunion."

"The whole thing is a miracle."

"Yes, no doubt about it. And now that you three are here, we are all praying that you will stay."

"You want John and me to stay with Joshua?"

"Of course, we do." She gave a laugh. "Having the famous pirate, Long John Silver, living here is better than having the long-lost war hero, William Wallace."

"Thank you, Mary. This is too kind of you."

"It's not my doing, Elizabeth. Lady Jane gave Clive and me strict instructions that we invite you to be a part of our family." She gave Elizabeth a hug. "Besides Clive and me, we have two cooks, four maids, and four men who shepherd the sheep and tend to the grounds."

"How long have you been here?"

"Clive and I have been here for these two decades—since before Elaine and David were married and left for America. The rest of the staff has been here for around ten years." She gave a quiet laugh. "They all married each other, and now there are a dozen little ones running around the grounds."

"It will be good to finally have a family."

"Hey, you two!" It was Silver. "Clive has been telling us about all the famous people who have spent time in this castle. He said that Sir William Bruce received Mary Queen of Scots in this very room two-hundred years ago, and that Sir Andrew Bruce hacked off the hands and head of Richard Cameron after the battle of Airds Moss."

"Aye!" Joshua came to John and pointed back at the armory. "You have to see all the swords and suits of armor!"

"You three go ahead. Mary and I are enjoying our new home at a woman's more leisurely pace."

"Our new home?" John stepped toward the two ladies. "What does that mean?"

"It means that Lady Frederick insists that you and I move in and live here for as long as we want."

"Oh, my." John just looked at the two and nodded his approval. "I wish Lady Jane was here so I could thank her properly."

"Mary tells me that she will be here in a week. We can thank her properly then."

Silver turned to Mary. "What about Captain Archer and his twelve men? Should I tell them to return to Edinburgh?"

"Oh, no, Mister Silver." She pointed west. "We have several cottages on the property. Once the *Remora* is secured, they are all welcome to come and join the staff if they want."

☠ ☠ ☠

Within a month, four of *Remora*'s crewmen fell in love with young women from the nearby towns of Bulmullo and Saint Andrews, and Joshua began to descend into a doldrum of depression. Elizabeth recognized the condition first, and brought her concern to her husband. She found John in the study with papers strewn about.

"John?" She stepped to the desk and picked up two sheets of paper from the floor.

"Can you take a break from your memoirs?"

"Of course, I can." He set down his quill and held up the sheet of paper. "When Jane asked me to do this, I was…"

"I know." She took the paper and read quickly. "Oh. This is good."

"And most enjoyable." He gave a stretch. "You wanted to talk?"

"I am concerned about Joshua."

"Oh?" He took back the page. "Is something wrong?"

"This life that you and I find so gratifying is wearing him down."

"But he told me that he enjoys the bird shooting and the horse riding. What have you seen?"

"He sits alone sometimes for an hour of more." Betty took a large breath. "He is eating less and he's losing weight."

"So, you think it's time for me to tell him about his letter of marque?"

"Yes." She paused. "I know it will hurt Lady Jane to see him go, but she's a reasonable woman. I know that like you and me, she would want the best for Joshua."

"I saw him at breakfast but not since. Do you know where he is?"

"He took the carriage and left. He said that he will be back late tonight or tomorrow morning."

"This isn't good."

Just then, Clive gave a light knock on the door jam.

"Yes?"

"There's a man hare to see you, Mister Silver. His name is Niles Tucker, and he claims that he works for you."

"Ah!" Silver pushed up and stepped toward the door. "Show him in!"

"Good afternoon, Captain." Niles was a man in his late twenties, with a strong body and attractive features. He held an Irish flat cap in his hands. "I have good news, sir."

"You found Rebecca Keyes?"

"Yes." He looked at Betty. "Am I free to speak, sir?"

"Of course, Niles." He swept a hand toward is wife. "You know my wife. I want her to hear everything you have to tell me, so you may speak freely."

"I am pleased to see you again, Elizabeth." He stepped across, took her hand, and kissed it. "Your husband has nothing but praise for you."

"Ha! Finally, a true gentleman in the castle." She picked up a glass. "We're having our afternoon sip of whiskey. Would you like to join us?"

"Oh, yes."

"It's a single malt whiskey made right here at our stills." She filled the glass. "So, tell us about Rebecca Keyes."

"She's in Bridgeton as we speak. It's a small town on the outskirts of Glasgow."

"Oh?" Betty handed him his drink. "What is she doing there?"

"It's a complicated story, Ma'am, so it's important that I tell you everything from the beginning."

"Then take a seat and tell us."

"My search began in Charles Town where she and Joshua were sponsored. It was public record that she was sponsored by a Doctor Peter Fayssoux. After two-and-a-half-years, a King's solicitor came to Charles Town and paid double the price of her remaining four-and-a-half-year obligation. It was a terrible day for both Rebecca and the other servants when the man took her away."

"Where was she taken?"

"I asked the doctor, but he explained that the solicitor was given strict instructions by his employer that his name and location be kept a secret."

"How did you find her if the doctor didn't know?"

"As I was leaving, the housekeeper told me about the day she left. She said that a local fishmonger named Samuel Paine came that same day to ask the doctor how much he would have to pay to free Rebecca from her remaining obligation so they could marry. When she told him that Rebecca had been sold and just left, Samuel ran to the docks where he saw her boarding a sloop that was moored a furlong from shore. He called to her, but she didn't hear him."

"He saw the name of the sloop, didn't he?"

"Yes—the Liberty—and that's how I discovered that it was registered in Boston and owned by British Army Coronel Francis Faulkner—the owner of a large textile mill at Acton."

"Is he here with Rebecca?"

"No. He was one of the Minutemen who died of his wounds after the battles at Lexington and Concord."

"Go on."

"Evidently, Captain Faulkner was a widower, and sent his solicitor to Charles Town to find him a new wife—a woman that was both his deceased wife's age and with her southern upbringing."

"So, Rebecca Faulkner is now a widow."

"Yes, and when I finally found her, it was at the ticket counter of a shipping company at Boston."

"Oh?"

"I bought a ticket on the same ship, and during the five weeks en route to Glasgow, we became close friends."

"This is all so fantastic." Betty took John's hand. "Please go on."

"Now that I am in her confidence as an advisor, I have accompanied her to every negotiation." Niles took a sip of his whiskey. "Mm—delicious."

"Where is she now, and when will she return to Boston?"

"When I left her, she was meeting with several Cheviot sheep herders to establish the importation of wool to her Acton mill, and buying several mechanized looms and the new Spinning Jenny's."

"Did she ask you your business here in Edinburgh?"

"I told her that I had a friend I needed to see." He took another sip of his drink.

"Being her confidante, may I assume that you will be buying the tickets for the return trip?"

"I have already purchased our tickets."

"Then you know the ship's name and the approximate departure date."

"She's the merchantman *Nancy* out of Portsmouth. After a stop at Liverpool, she will come to Glasgow at the end of October or the beginning of November. She was the only merchantman bound for Boston at that time."

Betty leaned forward. "A personal question, Niles."

"Yes, Ma'am?"

"You are a very attractive young man. Is Rebecca showing any signs of…"

"No." He shook his head. "I told her that I am married."

"Good."

"I have a question?"

"Sir?"

"How is the money that I advanced you holding up?"

"I have more than enough, sir."

"Very well." He took a piece of parchment from the desk. "I must write a letter for you to take back to Glasgow."

"Are you writing to Miss Faulkner about Joshua?"

"No—it's to General George Washington at Charles Town."

"You can trust me to hand deliver it, sir."

"No. It must be sent aboard the first ship leaving from Glasgow so that it reaches him at least two weeks before the *Nancy* arrives." He turned to Betty. "It will take me a half hour, Betty. Take our guest down to the kitchen and see that he gets something to eat while I write my letter?"

"Of course." She stood and gave Niles a smile. "Shall we?"

"Yes. I am starving." Once alone, John Silver sat down and penned his letter.

Dear General Washington,

As I am certain you remember, I told you the story of how Joshua Smoot and his betrothed, Rebecca Keyes, were separated at sea—he to slavery in Cuba, and she to her sponsors in Charles Town. It has been many years that the two have hoped and prayed to be reunited. Now that Joshua—John Manley—is in your service as a privateer, I have both good and bad news. The bad news is that Rebecca was widowed in the Spring when her husband—Acton Captain Francis Faulkner—was injured at the battle at Lexington, and died a week later from his wound. The good news is that Rebecca will be aboard the Brigantine Nancy, and will be leaving Glasgow on or about the first of November bound for Boston. Please assign John Manley to intercept that ship.

Your friend and servant,

Long John Silver

☠ ☠ ☠

Joshua returned from Edinburgh the next day, and after his obligatory greetings with John and Betty, he spent the afternoon alone in his study. Just before dinner, John came to him with an envelope.

"Are you alright, Joshua?"

It took the young man a moment "With everything I have, I should be the happiest man in the world."

"Then what is it?"

"Men work and strive all their lives with the hope that someday they can slow down and rest from their labors."

"But look at us, Joshua. We have that right here."

"I know, but I am not ready for it."

The two fell silent for several minutes. Finally, John put a hand on the envelope. "You have asked me several times about my meeting with General Washington, and I have always dodged the question."

"What have you been keeping me?"

"Patience, my friend." John stepped to the sideboard and poured two glasses of whiskey. "Here."

Joshua took his drink and looked up at the old man. "I'm listening."

"Before the general and I could discuss the issue of a price for the *Silver Cloud*, Alex Forrestal became quite agitated—declaring that he would oppose paying me a single penny for a ship that he had built and paid for."

"I can't blame the man." Joshua gave a nod. "If I had built and paid for that ship, I would have felt the same way."

"The general called for a truce, and then we discussed the condition of the American military forces."

"I remember our talks before you sailed to Charles Town—that America needed a navy."

"The two *Silver Cloud*s are being fitted as fighting frigates as we speak, and will be renamed."

"How long will that take?"

"The general said that it would take too long, so I suggested that he form a navy of his own by issuing several letters of marque to the officers and men in his army who had experience at sea, and to assign them to any ship that could be equipped with cannons."

"That's what I've wanted for years—a letter of marque."

"He and Joseph Reed liked my idea, and that led to this." John pulled the parchment from the envelopes. "Read this."

Joshua took the document.

Letter of Marque

Resolved, that this Letter of Marque and Commission be issued to John Manley, and that I hereby appoint him Captain of such private Ships of War that he may at times command, and that under his leadership, be engaged for the purpose of making Captures of British Vessels and Cargoes, and that he shall apply for the fame, and execute the Bonds which shall be sent with the said Commission.

I certify that from the testimony of the General Officers under whose orders John Manley acts, that he is brave and intelligent, and in all respects has supported the character of a Gentleman and man of honor.

Given Under my hand this 17ᵗʰ day of October 1775.

G. Washington

Chief of the Continental Army

"Damn you! Why didn't you give me this when you returned from Charles Town?"

"Because the timing was wrong."

"Wrong? You knew that I wanted this! You knew about my trouble with Governor Wright—that he refused to grant me such a letter!"

"General Washington didn't have any ships yet."

"I could have helped him find them!"

"Calm down, Joshua, and listen to me." Silver took a sip of his whiskey. "If I had given you that letter in Savannah, you would not have come here to Scotland. You would have never proved yourself a Marquess. Lady Jane would have never found her grandson."

Joshua collected his words. "I want to go to America—to Charles Town and my destiny."

"That may be a problem."

"Oh?"

Several of his crew are in love with the local girls, and Captain Archer just married a girl from Edinburgh and is moving there."

"I can captain the *Remora*, and I can find my own crew."

"If you're serious about sailing to Charles Town, then the *Remora* is my gift to you." Silver gave Joshua a toothy grin. "May you have fair winds and following seas all the days of your life."

CHAPTER NINETEEN:
The Privateer Lee

*F*ive weeks later, the *Remora* arrived at the Charles Town shipyards of Alexander Forrestal. General Washington was at the docks overseeing the loading of ten carronades onto a brigantine. He walked behind the ship and he workmen and called to the approaching ship.

"Welcome to Charles Town, Captain Manley !" He shaded his eyes against the morning sun. "I was expecting you sooner than this."

"John Silver didn't tell me about my letter of marque until after we were at Edinburgh for a month!"

"So, tell me about Scotland while we walk up to the house."

"It's a beautiful place, with everything a man could want. Horses to ride. Pheasants to shoot. Fish begging to jump into your creel. Beautiful women looking for American husbands."

"Then why did you leave such a wonderful place to join me in this war?"

It took Joshua a moment. "I'm a titled Marquess. I own a castle and over fifty acres of very productive land. I have a family." He took several breaths. "But I was nothing but that proverbial canary that is trapped in a gilded cage."

"Now that you are here, let me tell you about my fledgling navy." They entered the Forrestal mansion and the general took him to the library. "I have found five ships that can carry cannons, and I have found five of my army officers who are sea captains." He touched a paper on the desk. "I have these two ships—the *Lynch* and the *Franklin*—ready for service, with these three others—the *Warren*, the *Harrison*, and the *Washington*—to follow as soon as we can fit them with cannons."

"I came here in the *Remora*—Long John Silver's present to me. It carries a dozen cannons and as many swivel guns." He held up his letter of marque. "I can be your sixth captain and the *Remora* can be your sixth ship."

The general gave a nod. "Do you mind if I change the name of your ship?"

"The name isn't important, sir."

"Then you will be Captain John Manley, master of the schooner *Lee*."

"The *Remora*—the *Lee*—is ready for service, except for a crew."

"Yes." He looked back toward the dock. "I saw several women aboard. I assume they are the new brides of several of your men."

"Aye. Only four of the crew have shown interest in fighting the British."

"So, you'll need four dozen soldiers from Colonel Glover's Marblehead Regiment."

"And when I get those men, what are your orders?"

"Your mission will be to take any British ship you can, and if it contains arms and other military supplies, to deliver them directly to me and my troops at Boston." The general handed Joshua a box. "Here is your flag."

Joshua removed the lid and pulled out the white banner. In the center was a green Pine tree and the words, APPEAL TO HEAVEN. He looked up at the general.

"Colonel Joseph Reed—my new Military Secretary—chose that design. Do you like it?"

"Most appropriate."

"When do I sail for Marblehead?"

☠ ☠ ☠

The newly named *Lee* arrived at Marblehead, Massachusetts on 20 October and was met by Captain William Coit, the captain of the privateer *Harrison*.

"So, you're John Manley?" The young man stepped aboard and offered his hand. "The general didn't tell us anything about you except that you brought your own ship."

"That's about all there is. I'm a patriot and I'm here to serve."

"So, this is the *Lee*?" Coit walked from the stern to the bow. "I like the red sails. It gives her a threatening look."

"Threatening enough that I won't have to send a ball across any of the Brit's bows?"

"That, and possibly your twelve guns run out for battle if they try to ignore you."

As they spoke, Joshua's crew of twelve assembled on the deck. "Captain?" It was the first mate. "Jonny and I are staying aboard, but the four married men are asking if they can be paid and released."

"Is the ship secured?"

"Aye." The man looked around at the others and received nods. "Everything is secured, sir."

"You four are released." He pulled his purse from his pocket and handed each man ten pounds in coin as they passed with their wives.

"General Washington told me that I will be receiving fifty men from Glover's Marblehead Regiment. Do you know when they will arrive?"

"The first week in November, and as soon as they are trained them for service, we are to launch."

Joshua looked toward the nearby buildings. "Are there shore facilities I am to use, or should I plan on living aboard the *Lee*?"

"We have a building across from the docks for our military duties, but there are no beds or other comforts." He pointed. "When you're ready, you can begin reading the service records of your assigned crew."

The next morning, Joshua began reading the fifty records. Three of the men had been punished for fighting, but the accompanying letters from Colonel Glover gave assurance that the men had done their penance and were changed.

On November 9th, the *Lee* and the *Harrison*—both flying the Pine Tree flag—set sail to take their first British ships, centering their search on any ship headed for Boston Harbor where the King's troops were garrisoned. On November 12th, the *Lee* intercepted and took the British sloop *Polly*, then two days later Joshua took the British schooner *Pantages*. When these two prizes were delivered to Marblehead on the 20th, General Washington handed Manley a sealed envelope.

"What is this, sir?"

"I have received intelligence that the British Brigantine *Nancy* out of Portsmouth will be stopping at Liverpool and then depart Glasgow for Boston in late October or early November."

"Do you suspect them of smuggling arms to the British garrison?"

"Since they are out of Portsmouth, it is a strong possibility, so I want you to intercept them as far away from Boston as possible."

"You can count on the *Lee*, sir."

On November 28th, the privateer *Lee* intercepted the Brigantine *Nancy* seven leagues out of Boston. Although the *Nancy* carried six cannons, she immediately spilled her sails, turned her bow into the wind, and hoisted her signal flags to welcome the *Lee* to come across.

"Interesting." Joshua ordered three boats and a dozen armed men to accompany him to board and inspect the *Nancy*. Twenty minutes later, Joshua climbed to the deck of the *Nancy* where he instructed half his men to conduct a search of the British vessel.

"Welcome aboard!" The middle-aged man gave a curt salute and offered his hand. "I am Captain Hugh Montgomery. I didn't expect you to meet us this far from Boston, but being that you are here, I look forward to you piloting the *Nancy* to our assigned dock at Boston Harbor."

"You were expecting the Boston Pilot?"

"Of course, sir." He looked to the six men Joshua had sent away. He looked back to Joshua with a furled brow. "If you are not the Boston Pilot, then who are you?"

"I am Privateer Captain John Manley! I am operating under General George Washington's letter of marque with the purpose of taking for prize all British ships bound for Boston Harbor. My men and I mean you no harm unless we discover contraband among your cargo. A prize crew will convey you to the port of Beverly, Massachusetts. When you reach that place, you will be questioned and then released."

By now, all the passengers and most of the crew had assembled on the deck behind their captain. Joshua jumped up onto a deck vent and raised his voice. "As most of you probably know, the British army is building their garrison at Boston. I am convinced that most of you would agree with me, that we share the belief that we should be free to preserve the lives of our loved ones, ensure our personal liberty, and to protect our property from a foreign government that wants to take away those God-given rights!"

"You're a traitor to the King! What do you know about rights?"

"Who said that?" Joshua looked around at the crew and passengers. "Whoever it was, he is ignorant of what it is to be a free human being."

"It was me!" It was a young man in a badly-fitting suit. "You're just a pirate! How could a man like you—a man who commits piracy against his fellow countrymen—know anything about life, liberty, or property?"

"I have been a slave—sold on the block next to an African who the Mohammedans stole from his country. I was cheated out of—"

"Captain Manley! It was Tommy MacKay, one of the searchers. "You need to come down to the cargo hold to see something."

Joshua turned and looked down at the young man. "What did you find?"

"Please, Captain. You need to see this for yourself."

"Very well." He turned to the others. "Watch them. I'll be back as quickly as possible." Joshua followed the man down to the cargo hold where Tommy stopped and pointed at the row of bales.

"There, sir." Each of the bales measured the standard eight by eight feet.

Joshua looked about at the twenty bales. "It looks like a normal shipment of wool, Tommy."

"Take a handful of it, sir."

"Okay." He stepped forward and pulled loose a hand-full of the white material. "This is cotton." He turned to Tommy. "America ships cotton to England to be woven into cloth. "England never ships cotton like this to America."

Tommy walked to the side of the bale and pulled open the panel he and the others removed during their inspection. "Look inside the container, sir. There are hundreds of pistols in this one." He turned and pointed across the deck. "That one holds boxes of pistol shot, and the other ones hold barrels of gun powder." He beaconed for his captain to follow to another one. "This one has a thirteen-inch brass mortar."

"Now I know why General Washington ordered us to take the Nancy." He returned to the main deck just in time to watch a small boy drop his wheeled horse—one that looked much like the horse Joshua called TROY—and followed it across the deck to the foot of one of his men. The man reached down and caught the lad by the arm, grabbed the toy, and threw it over the side into the sea.

"Hey!" The boy bit the man on the forearm.

"Damn you!" The crewman gave the boy a rough shake and a backhand to the face that sent him to the deck in tears. "Bite me, will you?"

The boy's mother screamed and attacked the man like a banshee. Instinctively, the crewman pulled his pistol and pointed it at the woman. "You'll die for that, wench!"

As the man raised his pistol and pulled back the lock, Joshua ran to him just in time to deflect the shot upward with his sword.

Joshua put the blade to the man's throat. "If you had killed that woman, I swear by John Flint's black heart you'd have died before you could take another breath!"

"Joshua Smoot!"

He turned at the voice. "I'm Privateer Captain John Manley!" He looked at the several women crowded together. "Who called me that name?"

"Me!" Rebecca stepped forward, held up her left hand, and touched the farrier's nail on her thumb. "I'm Rebecca Keyes, the girl for whom you indentured yourself six years ago! The same girl who sent you into chains and slavery!"

"Becky?" He pushed the man away and rushed into Rebecca's waiting arms. After a deluge of kisses, he pulled back and stared at her, unable to believe what he was seeing. "John Silver is right. There is a God and he has answered our prayers!"

"I tried to convince you of that years ago at my secret garden."

Joshua turned to his men. "I'm taking Miss Keyes back to the *Lee*." He turned to the man who slapped the boy. "This one is to be put in irons, and the ship will be sailed to the port of Beverly."

"Aye, aye, Captain Manley."

When Joshua and Rebecca reached the *Lee*, they informed the bosun what had happened. "I am taking this woman to my cabin. We are not to be disturbed."

"Pardon me asking, sir, but is she somebody important—somebody the general asked you to arrest?"

"No." He gave her a kiss on the cheek. "This is Rebecca Keyes. We were to be married six years ago, but some evil men tore us apart, and the good Lord has seen fit to bring us back together."

"Very well, Captain." The man gave Rebecca a salute. "Welcome aboard the privateer *Lee*, Ma'am."

Once alone in his cabin, Joshua kissed Rebecca several more times, and then pulled back. "Where have you been all this time?"

"I'm the widow, Rebecca Faulkner. My husband was shot at Lexington last April and died several days later of an infection." She laughed. "So, now the bastard son of John Flint is a privateer captain working for George Washington?"

"I'm not the bastard son of John Flint, and I have the proof."

"Really?"

"There's more." He showed her the ring. "I'm Scottish royalty— the son of David and Elaine MacBride, the Marquess and Marchioness of Earlshall Castle near Edinburgh, Scotland." He gave her a questioning look. "Now it's your turn."

"I'm the owner of the Acton Woolen Mills, and I own three textile mills at Glasgow, Scotland just forty miles from Edinburgh." She gave him a push. "I am probably richer than you."

"I know this is a little late, but would you do me the honor of being my wife?"

"I thought you'd never ask."

"Yes, or no?" He gave her a push back. "You need to say the words."

"Of course, I will marry you." The two stood and looked at each other for several anxious breaths. "And you must promise me, Joshua, that you will never leave me again."

"But I'm one of General Washington's privateer captains, and there is a war coming."

"When you're not at sea, where do you live?"

"This ship is my only home."

"What about when the war is over? Where will you go then?"

"Uh…Savannah, where I was born and where my businesses are."

"But my home and mills are in Acton—fifteen miles west of Boston."

"Then, we have three homes to choose from."

"Three?" She gave a tilt of her head. "Acton, Savannah, and your castle in Scotland?"

"Yes, and I need to write a letter to John Silver. He'll want to know that I found you, and that we're to finally be married."

CHAPTER TWENTY:
Letters of Redemption

A courier from Edinburgh brought two letters on January 5, 1776 to the Earlshall Castle. One was from General George Washington and the other was from the newly-appointed Commodore of the general's privateer navy, John Manley.

"Here." Elizabeth handed John the general's letter. "Read his first, and then I'll read the one from Joshua."

He broke the seal, scanned the letter quickly, and then read it to her.

To my dear friend, John Silver,

I received your letter regarding Captain Manley and the widow, Rebecca Faulkner. A touching story indeed. I will alert him to the Nancy and her arrival date at Boston. I know this small favor will never begin to repay the generous gift you and Joshua gave to America, but I can hope it brings happiness to these two special Americans.

Your friend, G. Washington

Betty opened the second letter. She scanned down to the signatures. "Oh, my. This one is from Joshua."

Dear John and Elizabeth,

Miracle of miracles! I have changed my view of God. He has finally led me to my betrothed, Rebecca Keyes. She was aboard the Brigantine Nancy. We are to be married soon, and we will live at Savannah and Acton, which is near Boston. Someday, when God permits, we will come to Scotland to spend our declining years together with our children at the Earlshall Castle with you and Elizabeth. We will write after we are married and tell you the rest of our story.

By my hand,

Joshua Smoot

Commodore John Manley

John Silver took the letters from Elizabeth, set them on the desk, and took a sip of his whiskey. The two sat together for several minutes without a word. Finally, John turned to his wife.

"As I've told you since we met so long ago, I've always been a collector of favors. I'm not saying that the Good Lord is in my debt, but the way He has worked things out for us, I would never object to a person believing so."

"Careful, John. The Lord is listening, and you know that pride goes before a fall."

"No truer words were ever spoken." He took another sip of his drink, held up the glass, and looked at the rich amber liquid. "We will never know why He has done it, but He has given me everything that I have ever wanted."

"And those things are?"

"He brought Joshua and Rebecca back together."

"And?"

"He's given us this beautiful castle where we can live out our lives in luxury."

"And?"

"Aye—He gave me the Treasure of Dead Man's Chest."

"There's one more thing He's given you, John Silver—the most important thing you have."

"He's given me everything an earthly man could want."

"And?"

"Aye." He turned and gave her a kiss. "You're right, Elizabeth Silver. He gave me you—so much more than an old, black-hearted pirate like me deserves."

THE END

ABOUT THE AUTHOR

Commander Roger L Johnson was born in Los Angeles, California on January 29, 1944. At age nineteen, he was chosen for pilot training at the prestigious Naval Air Training Command where he graduated as the top student from his 57-man class. After three cruises to Vietnam aboard the aircraft carriers Ticonderoga, Enterprise, and Midway, Roger joined the fire service while remaining in the Naval Air Reserves. In 2001, he completed a 28-year career as a Crew Captain with Cal Fire at Klamath, California. Along with his extensive writing endeavors, Roger worked as a cartoonist for three separate magazine publishers. He is now known as the "Turtleman of Gig Harbor," having made and given away nearly a thousand turtles made from stones found on the beach. He and his wife Elizabeth live in Gig Harbor, Washington where he continues to write and create.

Printed in Great Britain
by Amazon

57687315R00089